THE BITTER BITE

THE BITTER BITE

Jeffrey Ashford

St. Martin's Press ⁂ New York

THE BITTER BITE. Copyright © 1995 by Jeffrey Ashford.
All rights reserved. Printed in the United States of America.
No part of this book may be used or reproduced in any
manner whatsoever without written permission except in
the case of brief quotations embodied in critical articles
or reviews. For information, address St. Martin's Press,
175 Fifth Avenue, New York, N.Y. 10010.

Library of Congress Cataloging-in-Publication Data

Ashford, Jeffrey.
    The bitter bite / by Jeffrey Ashford.
        p.   cm.
    ISBN 0-312-13931-4
    I. Title.
    PR6060.E43B58   1996
    823'.914—dc20   95-30036
                                                     CIP

First published in Great Britain by
HarperCollins*Publishers*

First U.S. Edition: January 1996
10   9   8   7   6   5   4   3   2   1

THE BITTER BITE

1

Diana stepped into the hall and faced the stairs. 'Penny,' she called out. There was no response. She turned and stared at the wall to the right of the Georgian table, inherited from her mother, where a small, rectangular hole from which wires protruded bore witness to the fact that the partial rewiring of the house was taking far longer than promised.

She was about to cross to the passage which led down to the kitchen, when a key was inserted in the lock of the front door; a moment later, Penelope entered. 'There you are! I've been shouting for you.'

'I nipped down to Campbells to see if the book I ordered had arrived. They promised it would be here by now.'

'Then allow another week.'

'The pleasant woman with a bad scar on her cheek suggested a fortnight.'

They both had wavy, not quite curly, brown hair, high foreheads, blue eyes, slightly retroussé noses, full mouths, and long, graceful necks; the same low-pitched voices and slightly clipped form of speech; so there was no mistaking their relationship, yet it was equally obvious that each had her own personality.

The door of the sitting room opened and a workman in green overalls stepped into the hall. 'OK if I start work on that point?' he asked, indicating the one by the table.

'Quite all right,' replied Diana, her tone suggesting that the quicker the better. She spoke to her daughter once more. 'The Ashleys rang a moment ago. They're feeling

5

grey and want us to have a pot-luck dinner with them. You're invited as well, but I said you'd probably be out with Calvin.'

'Not tonight. He and Tim are at their reunion.'

'Of course! My memory is beginning to make a sieve look solid. So you'll come with us?'

'I can't. I met Pat in Campbells and she suggested supper and a gossip.'

'Who could resist such an invitation?' Diana smiled. 'Would I were a fly on the wall! . . . We can drop you at her place, but I don't know when we'll be back except that it's bound to be late and well after midnight. Pat will run you home?'

'She's lost her car. She met Adonis number eleven who yearned for a weekend in Greece and they stayed a month. By the time they got back, there wasn't enough in her bank to live on, let alone keep up payments on the car.'

'Even her own mother says she's not a very practical person. If she can't drive you back, you must get a taxi.'

'When I can walk it in ten minutes?'

'You know I don't like you to be on the streets at night.'

'Yes, Mother dear. There are unspeakable dangers lurking in every shadow.'

Did other mothers worry as much as she did? Diana wondered. Or were they able to convince themselves that dreadful things only happened to other families? 'A taxi back, please. I'll give you the money.'

Penelope liked the last word. 'It'll be a total waste.'

'Not for someone who spends every Friday the thirteenth in bed and even there breathlessly waits for the ceiling to fall in on her.'

'Sometimes you talk absolute nonsense!'

'Your father has always claimed that that is what first attracted him to me, because his working life was spent in the company of people who weighed every word . . . I must get back to preparing lunch. What would you like for sweet?'

'I weighed myself this morning and I've put on three pounds since Monday.'

'Suppose you hadn't, what would your order be?'

'Apple and rhubarb pie.'

'With double cream?'

'If I'd lost three pounds.'

'Let's both pretend that the scales are misreading.' She crossed the hall to the passage and the kitchen.

Penelope made for the stairs.

The electrician, on his knees, surreptitiously watched her climb up. At each step, he was able to see higher up her legs because her shortish skirt was full and movement made it flare out. Just before she reached the landing, he convinced himself that he'd caught a brief, exciting, tantalizing, frustrating glimpse of lime-coloured pants.

Despite their speed, Calvin double de-clutched without even a muted groan from the crash gearbox. He floored the accelerator. The leviathan cleft the air with all the subtlety of a battering ram as it gathered speed to the accompaniment of a primaeval bellow. They closed on the Escort which had passed them earlier with a derisory gesture from the skinhead in the front passenger seat.

With a corner ahead of them, Timothy wondered if it was any good calling on St Christopher? He decided it was probably too late. Calvin was going to throw that skinhead's contempt back, no matter at what cost. They drew out to pass. Seated high, Timothy could see the driver of the Ford and his expression of growing panic. If he'd been in the other car, he'd be panicking.

Calvin edged closer. The driver of the Ford, convinced he was about to be swatted off the road, did the only reasonable thing and braked hard. Calvin shouted with triumphant pleasure.

The corner was now dangerously close. Calvin braked, judged the footbrake on its own would not slow them sufficiently, reached for the outside handbrake and hauled on that. The back end of the car began to slide. He released the handbrake, used the wheel to meet the slide and they cornered with a skill that seemed completely alien to the reckless stupidity he had shown only a moment earlier.

'I'll bet those bastards need a change of underclothes,' he shouted. 'We passed them doing the ton.'

Timothy had caught a glimpse of the huge speedometer as thev'd passed and that had recorded seventy-two. But give it a couple of days and it would have been a hundred and twenty and Tim Birkin had reached out of his grave to clap . . . When Calvin had said he'd got rid of the Maserati and bought himself a real car, Timothy had imagined a Ferrari 456. So when he'd been shown the 4.5 litre Bentley, looking as if it had just come out of a showroom, he'd been more astonished than envious. Later, he'd realized he shouldn't have been surprised. Calvin had bought the Bentley because it had a racing history – not as illustrious as he boasted – and even a has-been yuppie would be impressed by its worth. He had not bought it with any sense of awed excitement at being privileged to taste one of the peaches from motoring's golden age.

Occupants of oncoming cars waved and an optimist even tried to take a photograph of them as they flashed past. Much more of this, Timothy thought, and Calvin would start acquiring a Queen Mother wave.

'I wonder if Shorty will be there?'

For the first time in many years, Timothy recalled Adams – over six feet tall even then – to mind.

'Someone said his family had been caught by Lloyd's.'

It had been Adams who had nicknamed Calvin 'the arriviste'. Timothy didn't doubt that Calvin hoped the rumour was true.

They entered a village in second gear even though the traffic was light – at the higher revs, their exhaust note mimicked a Spitfire at zero feet and their passage could only go unremarked by the totally deaf.

At the end of the village, traffic lights brought them to

a halt and pedestrians stared at them. Calvin was gaining full value for money, but for all the wrong reasons.

When Calvin had suggested they both attend the reunion, the first for their year, Timothy had said, impossible. He'd been unable to find a job for the vacation and he certainly was not going to ask his parents for the money.

'I'm paying.'

'And I'm staying.'

'Don't be such a stubborn bastard.'

'It's in my genes.'

'Are you trying to tell me you don't want to find out whether Sammy Makins has turned into an even bigger shit than he was?'

'I know the answer to that now.'

'Give your pride a rest.'

Was it Wilde who had said that he could resist everything except temptation?

The Old Boys' Association had recommended two hotels, chosen for their reasonable terms and their proximity to Hastbarton. Calvin had ignored the recommendation and booked them in to the Mayton Country House.

Timothy crossed the large room, furnished with luxurious taste, and stared out through the window at the immaculately kept garden, beyond which was the private nine-hole golf course. At some stage of the reunion – if given the chance, at several stages – Calvin would tell his listeners that no, they weren't booked in at either the Bell or the Crusaders' Hotel, they were staying at Mayton. Not at all a bad pub . . .

A relatively recent theory, reduced to elementary terms, held that a butterfly's flapping its wings in one part of the world could cause a hurricane in another. Far more believable was the proposition that what happened in the first ten years was of infinitely greater consequence than what happened in the next sixty. When Calvin should have joined Hastbarton School along with all the other

9

new boys, he had been ill with hepatitis, picked up on some exotic holiday. As a result, he'd arrived only after the others had suffered and survived the initiation rites, formed friendships, and begun to learn the arts of survival. This had immediately branded him an outsider – a branding that his own character had done much to deepen. Had he been able to hide his sense of arrogant superiority, had he learned that he was not privileged as of right, he might have had the sense to put his head down and weather the storm. But he hadn't. He had been bullied unmercifully. In desperation, he'd appealed to the staff for help but, made thick-headed by tradition, they'd believed that a little harassment was good for the character; he'd appealed to his father to take him away, but his father had been too busy trying to divorce his wife at the least cost to bother with minor problems.

By chance, one Saturday afternoon, Timothy had come round the corner of the smaller sports pavilion to find three boys jeeringly roughing up fellow erk, Calvin. Most of his year would have walked on, ignoring the incident, because intermediates and seniors did not bother themselves with erks. But from his father he had gained a respect for fair play that was almost adult in conception, and even if the victim was the arriviste, he was sufficiently annoyed by the unfairness to join in on Calvin's behalf. Every erk knew the savage penalty of opposing his betters. The three had hastily broken off the engagement and retreated.

With the sharp intuition which Calvin sometimes possessed, he had understood why Timothy had gone to his defence. And with considerable cunning, he had appealed on the grounds of persecution for continued protection against his overwhelmingly numerous tormentors. Concerned, while reluctant to break with tradition, Timothy had finally and reluctantly come to the decision to provide this. And since he'd been a noted cricket and a good rugby player, and the fives champion while still only an intermediate, his influence had been considerable in a school which still held prowess at games to be on a par with, or superior to, academic achievement. The fact that there had been some who had hinted at dark reasons for his protection of Calvin had merely made him laugh . . . Initially, he'd regarded Calvin much as he would have regarded a puppy eager for reassurance, but then he'd discovered that there was an amusing companion beneath the arrogance. And not to be overlooked had been the Lucullan food hampers which Calvin's stepmother-to-be had sent with warming frequency . . .

2

It had started as always — a wild thought that had been triggered by some erotic possibility. The first thing he'd noticed about her was that her skirt was so short that if she bent down to pick up something, there was a chance he'd be able to see right up to her bum.

He'd watched her turn and had noticed how her dress had briefly tightened across one breast. He'd imagined his hand sliding inside that dress and fondling smooth flesh. When her mother had gone into the kitchen and she had climbed the stairs, he'd caught a glimpse — now he was certain of this — of lime green pants. He'd imagined his hands reaching under them . . .

In his mind, he asked her out for the evening and she accepted. As she went to sit on the pillion of his bike, she was careless how much he saw as she lifted her leg up and over. The evening was assured. A couple of drinks, a kiss, a hand that was not repulsed, a muted groan of desire as he fondled . . .

Burrell knew bitterness as reality rushed in. Make even half an advance and she'd rebuff him with contempt. He'd learned all about jeering rejection. Mabel, nicknamed Always-able, had told him that when she sought a bit of fun, she didn't want someone who stank like last year's polecat. It wasn't his fault that his breath stank. He'd been to umpteen doctors; he'd been to umpteen dentists.

He'd bet a fortune she was a gold medallist in bed. She wasn't exactly beautiful, not in the way some of the women on the telly were, but a man could never miss the volcanic promise of her body . . .

Thoughts of warm, moist flesh brought back memories he spent so much time trying to forget. Mabel had been a big, strong woman and she hadn't calmed down until he'd put a knife to her throat. That had scared her so much that her face had become quite twisted, making her look different. That he could cause such terror had made him feel ten feet tall. Would Penelope struggle so that he'd have to put a knife to her throat? To see a woman of her class that terrified . . .

He recalled her conversation with her mother. He visualized her return in a taxi. She climbed out, paid the fare, crossed the pavement, opened the wrought iron gate and stepped into the front garden (part of which was in shadow because of the high brick wall). As she began to walk up the flagstone path, he pounced. Shock and fear held her quiet whilst he gagged her. Once he'd pinioned her arms, he began to explore her flesh. Now, it didn't matter if his breath smelled or that he sweated so profusely (Enid: 'If I'd wanted a shower, I'd have used clean water').

There was pleasure to be gained from planning, even if only for a fantasy. He'd leave his Kawasaki a street away. He'd carry a knife, a gag, cord, a mask, and a condom to make certain he couldn't be identified from his semen. Afterwards, he'd burn everything burnable and throw what wasn't into the sea. He was clever. The police had never suspected him of the rape and murder of Mabel . . .

He left his dreams to return to his mean ground-floor flat in the slum area of Southwold which smelled of dirt, decay and him. He crossed to the table and searched amongst the litter for an unopened can of lager, but all the tins were empty. He swept several cans and an over-flowing ashtray on to the floor. As he watched one of the cans roll to a stop by the side of the television, he saw the Danish magazine he'd bought a couple of days before. He went over, picked it up, and turned the pages, knowing what he was going to see, yet – absurdly – sweating because of excited tension. When he reached page ten, he was surprised to discover that one of the two women now reminded him of Penelope. He imagined himself in the position of the second woman . . .

In one of the drawers of the old and battered chest in the bedroom was a ski-mask which he had been given some time before by a man who'd said he'd heard he was an ardent skier; one more contemptuous joke at his expense. In the kitchen were several knives. Any lengthy piece of material would make a gag. He always had a good supply of condoms because one never knew. String was better than cord if drawn really tight . . .

He looked at his watch. Eight-fifteen. Almost certainly a long time before she returned home. Time that could turn fantasy into fact . . .

'It is,' said the assistant headmaster, a tall, thin, cadaverous man, 'my duty and my pleasure to propose the toast.'

'Wouldn't you rather eat it?'

The reunion had reached the stage of loud voices, unfinished sentences, and retarded humour.

He peered over the tops of his spectacles. 'Unless my memory betrays me, Miller Secundus. Some years ago, I believe I had cause to observe that your humour even then had not kept pace with your years.'

That earned a round of laughter and table-banging.

'It is my duty because I am the only person present in a position to propose the toast since I am the only one not of the class of seventy-five. It is my pleasure because no man can be granted greater satisfaction than to realize that he has helped to transform thoughtless youth into thinking man.' He looked down the table at Miller. 'I feel it would be churlish even to hint at the fact that there are times when such satisfaction has to be tempered by the knowledge that not every thoughtless youth has successfully made such tergiverzation.'

More laughter and applause.

'Many years ago, when the headmaster was away at a

conference, it fell to me to receive a prospective parent. He asked me whether I could realistically claim that by the time a pupil left Hastbarton, he had learned a single thing that was of practical use in the outside world. I answered him by pointing out the school motto: *De nihilo nihil*. A *magister ludi*, I told him, has equipped a young man for any circumstance in any age when he has taught him the true meaning of that.'

'He'll bore St Peter with his lousy Latin,' Calvin said, as he reached for the decanter of port. 'And I reckon that suit of his was made in the time of Tacitus. I suppose the poor old sod can't afford a new one.'

Timothy took the decanter from Calvin and refilled his own glass. People gained satisfaction in odd ways.

Burrell crossed the pavement to his street-parked Kawasaki Z1000 and put the small bundle in the right-hand pannier. He unlocked the padlock, slid the chain free of the front wheels and put chain and padlock in the left-hand pannier. He felt the sweat break out across his chest and back.

The engine started at the first press of the self-starter. The ex-police bike was thirteen years old and had been in a clapped-out state, but he was a clever mechanic as well as electrician and now it ran with jewel-like precision.

He drove through the mean streets to Framley Park, which acted as a boundary line – to the east, terrace houses, many directly fronting the pavement; to the west, detached houses set in gardens. Almost all his work was carried out in homes in the latter category and he hated the owners who had so much more than he; there'd been times when he'd fantasized his fixing the wiring so that in time it broke down and caused a fire which incinerated all those who lived in the house, but it was too easy to determine the cause of such a fire and the blame might land squarely on his shoulders.

A mile further on, he turned into Marchmont Road, slowed as he came abreast of number seventeen. The brick wall was high enough to prevent his seeing the downstairs rooms, but there was a light in one of the upstairs ones. A change of plan or a light left on to suggest occupancy? He rode on. If he had been playing it for real, now he'd park his bike in one of the adjoining roads . . .

He turned right, then right again into a road of Edwardian houses, built before the need for garages had been appreciated; many of the owners had preferred not to lose part of their front gardens to garages and their cars were parked in the road with the result that a motorbike would surely go completely unremarked? He turned in to the pavement, between a Rover and a Saab. If he were playing it for real, now he'd switch off the ignition, secure the chain, retrieve the bundle, and walk down the road, helmet in one hand, bundle in the other . . . He cut the ignition, pulled the bike back on to its stand, secured the chain about the front wheel, brought out the bundle, walked down the pavement. Breathing had become laboured as if his chest were under pressure; sweat trickled down his cheeks.

He turned the corner, told himself that he'd gone far enough, but then continued into Marchmont Road. As he walked along the pavement, he finally accepted that it was no longer a fantasy to be played out, it had become reality. His hands began to tremble.

Traffic was light; the road did not offer a short cut to anywhere and it was the time of the evening when people had either gone out or decided to stay at home. The sky had clouded over and there was no moonlight. The street lighting was little more than adequate. He was satisfied that no observer, unless close, would be able to identify him.

The wrought iron gate was, as he had expected, locked. A quick glance up and down the road showed empty pavements. He put down the bundle and his helmet, brought out a crude but effective skeleton key which quickly forced the lock. He opened the gate, stepped into the garden, closed the gate. There was a light downstairs; the one in

16

the upstairs room was still on. He walked up the flagstone path and rang the front doorbell. If someone were at home, he'd say he'd lost a treasured cigarette lighter and had they found one? There was no response.

He crossed the lawn to stand in the shadow of the wall. His chest was tighter, his heart was thumping harder, his throat was dry even though he was continually having to swallow, and his underclothes were damp from sweat . . .

3

Penelope could never make up her mind whether to envy Pat or feel sorry for her. To an outsider, Pat's life was a complete shambles, yet she seemed to enjoy even the crises with rare gusto. Penelope yawned. 'I'd better make tracks.'

'Will you come next week to meet Don so you can agree that he's the greatest Mr U?' Pat sat on the floor, surrounded by the litter of a life lived without order.

'Either Wednesday or Thursday. I'll let you know which.'

'Bring Calvin along.' She was silent for a second, then said: 'On second thoughts, that's not a good idea. He'll become objectionable because he's such a snob.'

'That's unfair.'

'But a stinking rich snob, which excuses everything. Someone said that his father's been listed amongst the hundred richest men in the country. Is that right?'

'I believe so.'

'I'll bet he's framed the list with his own name picked out in gold.'

'Why are you so bitchy about the family?'

'Because I'm poor. And because they're so damned arrogant. But I'll tell you something. Steven isn't going to be quite so arrogant if he finds out about Fenella.'

'How d'you mean?'

'Surely you know that she's having it on the side?'

'Don't be ridiculous.'

'Sweetie, open your eyes wide.'

'I just don't believe it.'

'Royalty has its portrait painted, so Steven decided his wife should be immortalized. He asked around and someone gave him Geoffrey's name. Geoffrey likes big business like I like chastity belts, but he was in one of his financial downs and had to accept the commission. Fenella turned up at his studio and by the end of the first sitting was giving him the come-on.'

'You're making it up.'

'Geoffrey told me that himself. He becomes very talkative post-coital.'

'An old man's wishful thinking.'

'Just occasionally you can be a bitch! He still hasn't seen forty. And why be so disbelieving? If you were married to Steven, wouldn't you need some light entertainment? . . . Maybe you wouldn't. You're so naïve about marriage.'

'Because I think it matters?'

'Because you believe it still exists. Hasn't Calvin ever mentioned the possibility that Fenella's doing the two-step?'

'No.'

'What boring pillow talk you must have. You know something? Fenella's going to have to be really careful. If Steven ever finds out she's giving free samples, he'll turn vicious. I hope you realize that Calvin will be like that? He'll reckon he owns you lock, stock and bum. No sucking the window cleaner's toes.'

'That's not an occupation I'm considering.'

'Because you've never dared read beyond the introductory chapter of any sex manual.'

Penelope laughed.

'Are you suggesting you're becoming educated? Tell me, how does Calvin like it best?'

'I'd hate to shock you.' Penelope stood. 'All right if I ring for a taxi?'

'Sure. If those bastards hadn't grabbed my car back . . . I explained I'd had to spend so much in Tenos I couldn't pay them for a while, but I'd do the best I could. They wouldn't understand.'

Penelope crossed to the table, skirting or stepping over the litter on the floor. She lifted the receiver, dialled. As she waited, she said: 'By the way, what happened to Bruno?'

'When we got back from Tenos I told him I was skint and he'd have to do some paying and he just laughed. So I kicked him out. Men have no manners.'

The connection was made and Penelope ordered a taxi. She replaced the receiver. 'I hope Don's more creditworthy?'

'He has an Irishman's gift of the blarney. Of course, he's a liar. Started off by telling me he'd a top job in the City. It turned out he'd been cleaning the windows of high-rise blocks. Money's such a bind. That's what makes Calvin so attractive. He thinks a fifty quid note is small change.'

'In some ways, that's a pity.'

'Are you serious?'

'It makes him seem . . .' She became silent.

'The arrogant bastard he is? But what the hell? Show me a man who's perfect and I'll have him in an armlock before you've blinked twice. And as Confucius says: Seek perfection if you're a saint, money if you're a sinner.'

'Which makes you neither a saint nor a sinner.'

'There's no call to become personal!'

The front doorbell rang.

'I'll be on my way.'

'Peaceful days and energetic nights. And don't forget, when you're Mrs Moneybags, I love being taken out to lunch at ridiculously expensive restaurants.'

Penelope went out to the tiny hall – almost as untidy as the room she'd just left – and unlocked the front door.

The middle-aged woman, wearing the company's jacket, said: 'Miss Hurst?'

'That's right.'

'And you want to go to seventeen, Marchmont Road?'

'Yes.'

The company had been formed only eighteen months before, but already it was highly successful. Owned by a woman, the cars were driven by women and only women or couples were accepted as passengers.

Penelope shut the front door, followed the driver to a red Rover, settled on the back seat. The drive was made in silence because it was company's policy that drivers should not initiate conversations, and Penelope was wondering if Fenella really could be having an affair with the man who'd painted her portrait? Calvin's father was certainly not a man of warmth and charm, but that did not mean he would be any the less hurt if he discovered that his wife was betraying him . . .

The car turned into Marchmont Road, slowed so that the driver could read the numbers, stopped. Penelope opened the door and stepped out. 'How much do I owe you?'

'One pound sixty, please.'

She gave the driver two pound coins.

'Thank you, Miss Hurst. Good night.'

As the car drove away, Penelope opened her handbag, brought out the key of the gate, inserted this only to find the gate was unlocked. She smiled as she swung it open; in the morning she would have the pleasure of pointing out that this time it was her parents who were at fault. It did not occur to her to wonder why, since they'd left by car, they'd used the small gate.

She stepped inside, shut the gate behind her, took one pace up the flagstone path. A length of material was wrapped viciously tight around her mouth, a knife pricked her flesh, and a man said, his words accompanied by a foul stench: 'One sound and I'll slit your throat.'

Shock scrambled her mind.

'On the ground.' He dragged her down and she fell the last foot to jar her hip.

'Turn over.'

It had to be a nightmarish delusion, her mind silently shrieked. A hand gripped her and roughly rolled her over.

21

She tried to scream, but the gag distorted her mouth and left her unable to do more than make a muted, animal noise. The knife pressed down on the side of her neck.

'Another sound and you're dead. Get your hands behind your back.'

She was too terrified to act. One hand was grabbed and jerked behind her back with a savage force that ripped her shoulder with pain. She moved her other arm. Her wrists were tied with string.

He rolled her over on to her back. Terror made him ten feet tall. His face in the poor light was that of some monster with white, glaring eyes and cheeks; one small light of reason told her that he was wearing a mask. Behind him, outlining him, was her house – sanctuary so close that it mocked.

He squatted by her side, pulled up her skirt and ran his hands up her legs, making strange noises at the back of his throat as he did so. His fingers explored and once more she tried, and failed, to scream; this time, he did not put the knife to her throat. He pulled down her pants and threw them to one side, then stood. She knew a wild hope that he was a pervert who had already gained all the pleasure he sought. Then he undid his trousers and took them off, together with a pair of pants. He bent down, picking up something, stood; seconds later, he knelt and wrenched her legs apart.

Her mind divided. Although she knew what he was doing and suffered the mental and physical pain of his frenzied assault, she returned to one day that spring when she, Calvin and Timothy had gone for a walk and had come to a field left fallow and red with poppies; as she had passed through the poppies, she had trailed her hands across them, had felt the warm sun, had looked out at the time-softened countryside, and had known the certainty that here was a happy beauty that not even heaven could surpass . . .

4

'Is he going to marry her?' Geoffrey Hurst asked, as he changed up to third.

'I've no idea,' Diana replied.

'You haven't asked her?'

'If you'd moved with the times, sweet, you'd know that nowadays if a mother asks her daughter that question, she'll receive a rude answer. I suppose you're wondering whether to call him into the study and demand to know what his intentions are?'

'And if I did?'

'He'd laugh.'

'Damned if I can understand this generation.'

'Of course not. Part of your appeal is that you're a relic from the past.'

'Thank you.'

'It's a compliment.'

'I'm glad you've explained.'

'Only the other day, Cynthia said how wonderful it was to meet a man who opened the door for her.'

'I don't know that her approval counts for much.'

'She'd be very hurt to hear you say that . . . If it does lead to marriage, I hope he makes Penny happy.'

'Depends how closely he resembles his father. Steven swapped wives without any hesitation.'

'Sadly, that's rather become the habit.'

'But not with relics from the past.'

'Which is why our friends envy us.' She didn't care if that sounded smug. They had always regarded marriage

23

as a lifelong commitment and therefore had been able to cope with the inevitable strains that had arisen during theirs. She looked sideways at him. In the half-light, the lines of his face softened and he looked younger; almost the man she had married twenty-one years before. Not handsome, not someone to set the world alight, but the kind of husband a woman wanted when she'd matured sufficiently not to dream of Prince Charming . . .

'A penny for them.'

'I was thinking that you're not a bad catch for an old middle-aged woman.'

He let go of the steering wheel with his left hand and lightly touched her right thigh. 'A young middle-aged woman.'

'Very gallant! Very acceptable!'

He put his hand back on the wheel. They reached the top of Bank Street and turned on to the so-called inner ring road which, at that time of night, really did offer a quick route to the north-west part of town. 'I wish he weren't so very rich,' he said suddenly. 'It's difficult at her age to resist the charms of fast cars, yachts, and luxury holidays.'

'I think you're underrating her common-sense.'

'Pandora couldn't keep her hands off the box.'

'That was curiosity, not judgement.'

'Penny may be curious to know what the jet-set life is like once it becomes commonplace.'

'If she is, there's nothing we can do about it. We're just onlookers.'

'She might come to you for advice.'

'Very unlikely.'

He left the ring road and drove into an area of large houses set in large gardens. His inclination was to talk to Penelope, to find out how things stood, and advise; but he wouldn't do that because he respected his wife's judgement more than his own inclination.

Marchmont Road had been developed in the late thirties

and the houses were architecturally unadventurous, but solidly built from top quality materials. The heavy wooden gates were in as good condition as the day they'd been erected. He pressed the remote control and the doors opened. He drove in, coming to a stop in front of the garage doors. 'Penny can't be back yet.' Had she been, she would have opened the doors for them.

'I expect she and Pat have lost track of the time.'

'I don't know that I approve of her friendship with Pat.'

'It doesn't matter a damn whether you do or don't!'

He left the car, opened the garage doors, returned. 'I've heard one or two stories about her.'

'Which are probably only a little of what could be told.'

'Why d'you say that?'

'Her mother's not the most discreet of women.'

'Is she red-headed?'

'You're mixing her up with Claudine.'

He drove into the garage, switched off the engine and the lights. The street lighting hardly reached inside, but he was too conversant with the layout to be bothered and he moved confidently across to switch on the single overhead bulb.

They left the garage. He came to a sudden stop when halfway to the front door.

'Is something the matter?'

'I thought I heard an odd noise . . . What's that?'

She looked in the same direction and picked out amongst the shadows a shapeless mass.

'Has someone chucked more rubbish over the wall? I'd like to keep our dustbin full for a fortnight and then empty it in their garden.'

'Are you sure it's rubbish?'

'Now you mention it, it looks rather like someone. A drunk who climbed the wall and then passed out? Hang on and I'll go over and find out.'

He stepped on to the lawn and began to cross. He first confirmed that the form was human and then, when only a few feet away and she groaned, discovered she was Penelope.

5

'How could it happen?' Hurst demanded in a shaking voice.

All too easily, thought the PC; not cynically, just matter-of-factly.

'She was curled up on the grass, moaning. I thought she'd had some kind of a fit. Then I saw the state of her clothes and discovered her hands were tied and she was gagged . . .' Hurst turned away so that his tears should not be seen. After a while, he turned back. 'What happens now?'

'CID will have a word with her as soon as possible to find out how much she can tell them.'

'She's far too shocked.'

'I know it'll be real tough, but the quicker she's questioned, the better the chance she'll remember something useful. But you can be sure the doctors won't let anyone worry her until it's safe.'

Hurst walked over to the window and stared at the drawn curtains as if he were looking through them at the garden. 'Why don't you stop this ghastly sort of thing happening?'

'We do all we can to prevent such incidents.'

'Incident? Christ! She's my daughter and has been raped by some bastard and you call it just an incident?'

'Mr Hurst, it's like this . . .'

'We told her to come home by taxi because at night the roads aren't safe. But they'd be safe if you did your job . . . Then she's attacked in the garden. She can't be in her

27

own garden without being attacked. And all you can do is call it an incident . . .' He faced the curtain once more. After a while, he said: 'I'm sorry. I don't really know what I'm saying.'

The PC had often been cursed by a victim or a relative because he had not prevented the crime; only very seldom had he subsequently received an apology for such illogicality. That he did now, increased his sense of sympathy for the family and that threatened to break down the necessary barrier between himself and the tragedy. He was glad when the front doorbell rang. 'That'll be CID. I'll go and let them in.'

There was only DC Naylor – young, sharply-featured, and newly-awakened. 'I'm very sorry about what's happened, Mr Hurst.' His words were professionally formal; his tone held genuine sympathy. 'I'm going to have to ask you rather a lot of questions, so we might as well sit.'

Hurst settled on the settee. The PC looked inquiringly at Naylor, received a brief nod of the head, left. Naylor brought a notebook from one coat pocket, a ballpoint pen from his breast pocket. 'To start with, will you tell me what happened when you returned home.'

'I found her,' Hurst replied, with heartbreaking simplicity.

'Let's start when you turned into Marchmont Road; was that at the top or the bottom?'

Hurst had to struggle to bring his mind to bear on the question. 'We came in from Erroll Road,' he finally said.

'Was there much traffic moving?'

'No.'

'Were there any pedestrians?'

'I don't think so.'

'You can't be certain?'

'I wasn't bothering to notice. I didn't think . . . How was I to know what had happened?'

People who enjoyed the Hursts' quality of life still believed, consciously or subconsciously, that they were cushioned from almost all crime and so had not developed an early warning system. 'What did you do when you arrived here?'

'Drove in.'

'Were the outer doors shut?'

'Yes.'

'And locked?'

'Yes.'

'You're quite certain of that?'

'I had to use the remote control.'

Naylor wrote briefly. He looked up. 'And then?'

'I drove up to the garage.'

'Was that open?'

'No. Which was odd . . .'

'Why was that odd?'

'If Penny's back first, she opens the doors for us so that we can go straight in. We just thought she hadn't returned.'

'And after you'd garaged the car?'

'We began to walk round to the front door. And that's when I heard . . . I suppose I thought maybe it was a kitten. Then I saw what looked like a pile of rubbish.' He hesitated, added: 'Some time ago, kids threw rubbish over the wall. At least, I supposed it was kids. What makes them do such stupid things?'

'I don't think anyone knows the answer to that.' Naylor was used to witnesses trying to shy away from describing the moment when they'd discovered that crime had invaded their lives. 'Did you go across to see if it was rubbish?'

'When I could see it was a person, I thought it must be some drunk who'd climbed the wall and collapsed.'

'Or opened the gate first?'

'When we're all out, that's always kept locked.'

'How was your daughter lying?'

'She was all curled up, with her hands tied behind her and a gag round her mouth. Her skirt was up to her waist and she was bleeding . . .'

'Take all the time you need, Mr Hurst.'

He swallowed heavily, blinked rapidly. He'd never know for how long his eyes had told him what had happened, but his mind had refused to accept the fact. 'I called my wife across . . . We helped Penny into the house and I rang our doctor. He tried not to come out, but said we should drive her straight to the hospital. They aren't real doctors any more, just medical clerks . . .'

'What was your daughter able to tell you about the incident?'

'It wasn't an incident. She was raped. Do you understand? She was raped.'

'I understand very well, Mr Hurst. But usually it helps a little in this sort of case if we describe events in neutral terms.'

After a moment, Hurst said: 'I'm sorry.'

'No call for any apologies.' Naylor, as had been the PC, was surprised and disconcerted by the apology. 'Was she able to tell you anything?'

Hurst struggled to speak more coherently. 'She walked through the gateway after leaving the taxi and he attacked her before she had any idea he was there. He had a knife and threatened to cut her throat if she screamed. He gagged her and tied her hands behind her back, rolled her over and felt her. And then he took off his trousers . . . And all she remembers after that is the field of red poppies.'

'Do you know what she means by that?'

'No.'

'Could she describe the man?'

'I don't think so.'

'Did you search the garden around where you found her?'

'No.'

'Then you haven't removed anything?'

'No.' Then he remembered. 'My wife picked up my daughter's pants.'

'Where are they now?'

'I've no idea.'

30

'We'll need them for forensic examination.'

'No!'

'I'm very sorry, but they could furnish an important clue. Please make certain they're not washed before we have them.'

This indignity, so much smaller than that already inflicted on Penelope, distressed him almost as much.

'Mr Hurst, have you any idea who the rapist might be?'

'God Almighty, of course I haven't! If I had . . .'

You'd throttle him with your own hands, Naylor thought. 'Does your daughter have a boyfriend?'

'Yes.'

'How long have they been friendly?'

'Several months.'

'And before then she no doubt had other friends. I'll need their names, but you can give me those some other time. Just for the moment, though, can you think of any who might have been bitterly jealous when your daughter ceased to be friendly with him?'

'You think one of them would rape her?'

'It happens.' Human nature didn't change for the better as the income level rose. He looked down at his notebook. 'That seems to have covered everything for the moment, so now, with your permission, I'll take a quick look at the garden. We'll be back when it's light to make a more thorough search, so I'll ask you and your wife not to go anywhere but on the path.' He stood.

'Is it all right if I go to the hospital now?'

'Of course. We only had to ask you to stay so I could have a word with you. I very much hope you find your daughter is not too seriously injured.' He paused, then continued: 'She's going to depend a very great deal on you and your wife; your support can make a tremendous difference.'

'We'll give her all the support we can,' he said thickly.

'I'm sure it'll help . . . I'll see myself out and the constable will be leaving with me.'

A moment after the other had left the room, the carriage

clock on the mantelpiece struck the half hour. Hurst turned and stared at it. Half past three. It was beyond comprehension that only an hour and a half ago he and Diana had thought the world a happy and secure place.

6

Naylor and WPC Carmichael waited in the reception area of the hospital, only occasionally talking to each other. She was reading a copy of *Country Homes*; his thoughts were on his wife and the thousand and one complications that pregnancy brought . . .

'Detective Constable Naylor.'

He jerked his mind back to the present, stood, crossed to the information desk by the side of which stood a lanky, bespectacled man in a white coat. The receptionist introduced the doctor.

'We'll go through to one of the rooms,' Brooks said curtly.

As Naylor, and Carmichael, followed down a long corridor, he thought – on the sole evidence of his own prejudice – that Brooks was one of those doctors who believed God sat on his right hand. He'd begun to dislike doctors from the moment Hazel had become pregnant and had had to suffer her first examination.

They went into a room which, from the presence of several chairs, two tables on which were magazines, a coffee machine, and a noticeboard, they presumed to be a rest room for the staff.

'I'm very busy, so you'll have to be brief,' said Brooks.

Cock-of-the-walk in the middle of the night when the senior registrar was tucked up in bed. 'Can we have a word with Miss Hurst?' Naylor asked.

'Out of the question. She has been heavily sedated and

must be left in complete rest until the middle of the morning at the earliest.'

'How is she?'

'She suffered a couple of relatively slight cuts on the neck, bruising to both cheeks and about the mouth, bruising to one hip, severe bruising in the pubic area, and some internal injuries which we do not think are serious. It is too early to try to assess the psychological trauma she has suffered.'

'Has Dr Kent examined her?'

'He has.' Brooks's tone made it clear that the other's presence had been as unwelcome as it had been unnecessary.

'I'll be in touch with him, of course, but can you give an indication of his findings? Was Miss Hurst raped?'

'An absurd question.'

'Not really, Doctor,' Carmichael said. 'We do meet cases in which rape is claimed, but the medical examination proves that to be probably false.

'She was raped.'

'Did Dr Kent find any traces left by the rapist?' Naylor asked.

'I don't think so.'

'There was no semen?'

'No.'

Five minutes later, as they left the building and crossed to the car park, Carmichael said, her tone bitter: 'Even rapists have learned the wisdom of using condoms.'

Detective Constable Tyler had joined the force a naïve idealist which explained why, by middle age, he had become cynically certain that the devil had *all* the tunes and not just the best ones. Still capable of being shocked by man's inhumanity to man, he was no longer surprised by it; still surprised by the venality of those in power, he was no longer disturbed by it; still disturbed by the indifference of those with towards those without, he no longer believed in the possibility of equality. 'Nothing, Doctor?'

'Precisely nothing.' Kent was small, sharp, and aggressive. He was also an expert in sexual cases and brilliant at uncovering those traces which could identify and inculpate the guilty man or, occasionally, woman.

'He wore a condom, then?'

'Almost certainly.'

'And there were no hairs?'

'I have just said, I could find no traces.'

'Sorry, Doc. Just trying real hard to find something that'll help track down the bastard.'

Kent said, 'Of course.' He settled back in his chair, set behind a large desk on which were several files and a couple of thick text books. 'The only point of any practical consequence is that the nature of the bruising and the internal injuries suggest a degree of frenzy.'

'More than usual?'

'Sufficient to indicate the possibility of a man suffering from the so-called Belladrome-Styles syndrome.'

'What's that?'

'A classification which seeks to differentiate when in my opinion there is no justification for doing so. However,' Kent rested his elbows on the arms of the chair, joined his fingertips together, 'we may be dealing with a man of weak character, possessed of an over-active imagination, who suffers from some defect which prevents his readily being able to form relationships with women or – if homosexually orientated – other men. A prey to strong sexual desires, this failure exacerbates a sense of frustration. Frustration leads to fantasizing and in his fantasies he forces himself on someone who cannot reject him despite his disability. The fantasies fuel his desires, his desires fuel even more vivid fantasies; eventually he reaches the point where he is driven to turn fantasies into fact.'

'What sort of defect would set all that off?'

'The possibilities, either physical or psychological, are

virtually endless. Perhaps he was abused as a child, per-haps he's a stand-in for Quasimodo.'

'Who?'

'The hunchback of Notre Dame.'

Tyler was little the wiser. 'So if we turn up a suspect and he's only half his marbles or a face like a nightmare, we can start thinking we've found the rapist?'

'I suppose you might put it in such non-literary terms,' replied Kent, whose sense of humour tended to be ironic.

In her middle thirties, WPC Carmichael was a married woman with two children; she had been in the force since, at the age of twenty, she had sought work that she would find more rewarding than a secretary's. She was not clever, a good administrator, or even ambitious, but she possessed an inner calmness and a sense of sympathy that was obvious and this was why she was a valued member of the division and invariably called out in sexual cases when a woman was the victim.

'Can you tell me when I can have a word with Miss Hurst?' she asked.

The intern rubbed his long, pointed chin. 'That'll sharpen all the memories she's trying to blur.'

'I'm going to have to talk to her sooner or later.'

'I suppose so. All right, as short a time as possible and the nurse will cut it even shorter if she thinks that necessary.'

Five minutes later, accompanied by a nurse, she entered the room which contained two beds, only the nearer of which was occupied. 'Hullo, Miss Hurst. I'm Constable Carmichael. I do hope you're feeling a little better?' A potentially banal, perhaps even objectionable question – since to some it might appear to minimize the degree of suffering experienced – that became warmly sympathetic when asked by her.

'Yes, thanks,' Penelope answered briefly. There was bruising on her cheeks close to her mouth and a plaster on her neck, but the clearest sign of hurt was in her eyes.

'I'm very glad. I'm sorry, but I'm going to have to ask you questions if you're up to answering them – do you think you are?'

She nodded.

'If you find things becoming too distressing, just say . . . What I have to find out is how much you can remember, so will you tell me what happened from the moment you left the taxi?'

Penelope stared into the past and her expression became one of pain. After a while, she said: 'I paid the taxi, opened the gate, and walked into the garden . . .'

'Was the gate locked?'

'No. Which was odd. I just thought my parents had forgotten to lock it before they left. I told myself I'd rib Father . . .'

'Would you rather tell us some other time?' asked the nurse.

'I'm all right.'

It wasn't every woman who had the courage to fight her memories, Carmichael thought approvingly. 'What happened after you entered the garden?'

'I started to walk up the path and he grabbed me and wound something round my mouth. He put a knife against my neck and said he'd cut my throat if I screamed. He forced me down on to the grass and tied my hands.'

There was a pause. 'And after he'd tied your hands?' Carmichael asked quietly.

'He rolled me over.'

'Could you see his face?'

'First, I thought he was a devil, then I realized he had on a mask.'

'Can you describe the mask?'

'Only that it was white about the eyes and mouth.'

'What was he wearing?'

'It looked like a pullover and jeans. But he was in the shadow and I couldn't really see clearly and I was so frightened . . .'

'Of course you were. You're doing wonderfully well. What happened then?'

'He pulled up my skirt and felt me and he was making noises like a . . . like a dog. He pulled my pants off and stood and I thought maybe . . . But then he took his trousers off and did something with his hands . . .'

Probably rolling on the condom.

'And he forced my legs apart and . . . and the poppies were red and the countryside was so beautiful.'

'I'm sorry?'

'The most beautiful in the world.'

Carmichael looked at the nurse who indicated that it was time to bring an end to the interview. Carmichael was about to say goodbye when she remembered what Dr Kent had said to Tyler. 'Did you –?'

'That's enough,' snapped the nurse.

'Please, just one thing more.' She waited a moment, but when the nurse did not say anything, she spoke to Penelope. 'Did you notice anything unusual about him? Did he limp, was one of his hands malformed?'

'His breath smelled horrible. And he sweated all over me. I'll never be able to wash myself clean.'

'You're already quite clean,' said the nurse, with that brisk, professional conviction which was designed to breed belief in the mind of a patient.

As Carmichael left the room, she thought that heavy sweating didn't seem much of a hindrance to a happy sex life, but bad breath certainly did. She waited until the nurse had shut the door, then said: 'Have you any idea what she means when she talks about the poppies and the beautiful countryside?'

'None at all. She is still confused and your questioning will hardly have helped.'

'I know. But I had to talk to her if we're to catch the rapist.'

'Are you going to?'

'There's a very good chance we will.' She also had to express a confidence she did not necessarily feel.

7

A few years previously, Nick Rees had been driving along a major road when a car, in the hands of a fourteen-year-old joy rider, had come out of a side road, passing a stop sign, and slammed into the side of the Peugeot, sending it spinning off the road and into a tree. After weeks in hospital and months of further tests and consultations, he had been forced to accept the fact that his brain had suffered an injury which could not be identified; he would always be plagued by vicious headaches, dizziness, and frequent bouts of nausea, and that as a consequence he would be unable to return to the partnership; that his only course was to try to find accountancy work where the inability to do anything for two or three days at a time would not matter.

There had been financial compensation, but the income that this could generate had fallen far short of what he had been earning. The family's standard of living necessarily had taken a tumble. It was to their credit that they had accepted this with little bitter nostalgia. They had moved from the large Georgian house into a semi-detached; they had sold most of the antique furniture and Christine's jewellery, except for her engagement and wedding rings; he had resigned from the golf club, she had begun to buy her clothes at M & S; they had no longer gone up to the theatre in London, not even when Domingo had appeared in *La Bohème*; but there had been one economy which both had refused to consider and that was that Timothy should leave his public school for a state

39

one or that on gaining his A levels he should forego university and seek a job immediately.

Friends – they had been lucky with their friends because only a few had found reasons not to visit the semi-detached in one of the downmarket areas of the town – often told Christine that they didn't know how she coped. There were times when she didn't either and this was one of them. She nibbled her upper lip as she stood in the small hall and listened to the booming exhaust of the Bentley as it drew away from the pavement; she fiddled with a button on her print frock as a key was inserted and the front door opened.

Timothy dropped his suitcase and came forward to kiss her on the cheek. 'Hi, Chris.' None of them could now remember when, or why, he had started to call both his parents by their Christian names.

'Did you have a good time?' she asked, putting off the evil moment for a moment longer, even though this was the coward's way.

'Several of the blokes I liked were there, Old Maglud was in great form, the food wasn't even a distant cousin of the swill we used to get, and there was enough booze to float a battleship.'

'The last being the most significant?'

'Of course.'

'What was the hotel like?'

'Oil sheikh living. I reckon I could very soon get used to the lifestyle.'

'I wouldn't try, if I were you.'

It was so unusual for her to make any reference, however oblique, to their fortunes, that he said: 'Is something wrong?'

She drew in a sharp breath. 'I'm afraid so.'

His concern was immediate. 'Nick?'

'No. Penny.' Even now she was not certain exactly what were his feelings for Penelope. That he had always been very attracted to her, she had no doubt; that he now accepted the close relationship between her and Calvin was obvious; but how painful it had been, and was, to see Penelope and Calvin together was a question she could not answer.

'What's happened?'

'She was attacked in her garden last night.'

'Was she badly hurt?'

'She was raped.'

'Christ!' he said hoarsely. 'Where is she now?'

'I don't know.'

As he crossed to the telephone, on the white wood table, she returned to the kitchen and closed the door. She resumed de-pipping the Seville oranges she had bought the day before. Whatever physical injuries Penelope had suffered, they surely would be as little compared to her mental hurt. Did she have the mental toughness to overcome that?

The door swung open and Timothy entered. 'Diana says Penny's still in hospital. She's been injured, but not seriously. I asked if it was OK to see her and Diana said she didn't know if there were fixed visiting hours, but the thing to do was just go along. Is it all right if I borrow the car or has Nick got it?'

'When I heard about Penny, I said you'd want to see her as soon as you were back, so he took a bus.'

It was a measure of his worry that he didn't thank her for their thoughtfulness.

Art succeeded in making Fenella look almost as young as she claimed to be; the wealth of her husband made certain that her claim was not challenged, at least not in either his or her hearing. She had blonde, wavy hair, shapely eyebrows, deep blue eyes, a cheerful, snub nose, a full, curvy mouth with moist lips, and a dimpled chin; her complexion was English rose; thanks to rigorous dieting, constant exercise and skilled massage, she had a figure that could wear haute couture and not look twenty years too late.

She met Calvin in the great hall of Franklin Manor, a

41

vast, echoing space with suits of armour, stags' heads, and a fireplace almost large enough to roast the proverbial ox. 'Have you come straight here?'

'After leaving Tim at his place.' He dropped his pigskin suitcase on to the marble floor. Their relationship was on a remarkably pleasant basis, remembering his distress when his father had divorced his mother. But it was in both their financial interests to be seen to like each other.

'I'm afraid I've some terrible news.'

'Dad's ill?' he said, wondering just how this could affect him.

'It's Penny. She was returning home late last night and a man was hiding in the garden. He raped her.'

'Who?' he said thickly.

'I don't know if they've caught anyone yet.'

'The bloody bastard!'

He picked up his suitcase, crossed the hall, climbed the double staircase with elaborately carved balusters.

She patted a stray strand of hair above her forehead into place. He'd cursed the rapist, but not asked how Penelope was. His father's reaction would have been the same.

Detective Sergeant Grey was still in his early thirties, but already he had ceased to worry about his chances of promotion. The higher one rose, the more one became an administrator rather than a street detective. His appearance was both an asset and a liability. He was round in face and figure, to such a degree that before his marriage one of his lady friends had declared him to be more cuddly than Rupert Bear. To look at him was to feel like smiling and suspects frequently found themselves chatting when it was entirely in their interests to keep their mouths claptrap shut. But the very benignity of his appearance added more than a touch of woolliness and he often had to work hard not to be underrated.

As he sat behind the desk, he fiddled with a pencil. 'She can't tell us anything more than that.'

'Not according to WPC Carmichael; not at the moment, anyway,' replied Naylor.

He dropped the pencil, sat back in the chair. 'And the bastard was wearing a condom so there's no DNA print-out. Where do we go from here?'

'I've been thinking. The outside doors to the garage and the gate were locked and there were lights on upstairs and downstairs. As far as any casual observer could tell, the house was occupied by the family. So at that time of night, the odds had to be that no one would be leaving or arriving. Yet this bastard picked the lock of the gate, stepped into the garden, and waited in the shadow of the wall for quite some time.'

'You're suggesting that he knew the house was empty and the daughter would be returning first, on her own?'

'That's right.'

'How could he know?'

'Suppose the Hursts had workmen in during the day and one of them overheard the family talking; or someone called and was told they'd all be out that evening, but returning at different times?'

'Check it out.'

'Right. But it may be best to leave it until tomorrow morning when the Hursts might be more up to remembering?'

'That makes sense . . . If you haven't heard, there was no joy from the garden search. Footprints in the grass give a shoe size of ten or ten and a half and soles with a criss-cross pattern, but there were no peculiar marks so there's no chance of a positive identification. Knee prints suggest a jeans-type material, nothing more.'

'No condom packet?'

'No.'

'He certainly knew not to leave any traces behind. And that, added to the forcing of the locked gate, has to suggest someone with a record or at least with criminal connections.'

'It's possible.'

The receptionist tapped several keys of the keyboard of the desk-top computer, read the screen. 'Miss Hurst is in the Claymore Room. That's on the third floor of the west wing.' She pointed. 'Go over there and take the lift and turn right when you leave it.'

Timothy thanked her, crossed to a wide passage, halfway along on the left-hand side of which were two lifts, both in use. As he waited, he looked down at the bunch of tulips in his hand. They were red, which was not Penelope's favourite colour, but they had been all he could buy; on a Sunday evening, he'd been lucky to find anything.

He hoped he would not make a fool of himself when he first saw her. They'd initially formed a threesome, but Calvin's jealousy had soon made it obvious that the relationship must dissolve into a twosome and a good, but not too good, friend. The question had been, who was to be the friend? Had he been the complete fool to give in without a fight? But the years since his father's accident had taught him many things, one of which was that wishful thinking was no match for hard facts. He had been in a position to offer her nothing beyond his love; Calvin had been in a position to offer her luxury. Only a moonstruck fool, he'd told himself, could expect anyone as attractive and fun-loving as she to find the choice a difficult one . . . Some time later, she'd said something which had made him think she had been perplexed and hurt by his decision because she might well have made the opposite choice to the one with which he had credited her. But he hadn't asked her if this were so. It was soon after that that she'd finally agreed to go with Calvin to the latest in-resort in Mexico. During the time they'd been away, he had discovered just how tormenting jealous imagination could be . . .

44

The right-hand lift arrived, the doors opened and three men and two women left. He entered and was joined by a couple who were still arguing when he left them at the third floor. He quickly found a door marked Claymore Room, knocked and went in. Penelope lay on her back, eyes closed, her brown hair spread out on the pillow as if she had been posed for a sentimental Victorian art photograph, and he experienced an immediate sense of relief because her expression seemed calm and relaxed. But then as she turned her head and opened her eyes, he saw her expression change. He had rehearsed words of comfort, but what he said was: 'Oh, Penny!'

Tears welled out of her eyes.

He was proving to be a great comforter, he thought bitterly.

She reached under the pillows and produced a lace-edged handkerchief, with which she wiped her face. 'I'm sorry, but seeing you . . . I'm better for that little cry.'

He held out the tulips. 'I know the colour's wrong, but these were all that the old woman by the railway station had.'

'You've just made red tulips my favourite flowers.'

There were two vases on the nearer chest-of-drawers. He half filled one of them with water from the handbasin, put the tulips in it. He sat on the chair set close to the bed, cleared his throat. He wanted to ask her how she was, but was afraid that the circumstances might make it an embarrassing question for her to answer.

'I'm slowly coming to terms with things,' she said.

It was not the first time that she had answered his unasked question. Until Calvin had forced the break-up of the threesome, they had often found themselves on the same wavelength.

'One of the staff tried to give me some counselling earlier on, but she reminded me of my gym mistress and I couldn't stand the old cow.'

'The gym mistress or the counsellor?'

'Both . . . And that reminds me, how did the reunion go?'

'Very . . .' He stopped. It was hardly the time to say that it had been very enjoyable.

'For God's sake, stop being so careful. If it was great, it won't make things any worse for me. Did you see all your friends?'

'Quite a few of them.'

'And you spent hours boasting about what little devils you'd been?'

It had taken him long enough, but he finally realized that she wanted him to lift her away from the hospital bed and back to the world she had always known until the previous night. He let his imagination loose and painted the picture of a reunion that would not have been recognized by any of those who had been present at it.

8

Timothy switched off the engine and it died with an uneasy vibration that shook the car. The garage said that everything easily accessible had been checked and the only thing left was to strip down the engine and find out what was wrong. That day was being put off for as long as possible; when money was tight, delaying tactics had to be employed, even if the odds were that delay might lead to a far larger bill in the end.

Christine and Rees were in the sitting room, watching television; he cut the sound with the remote control. 'How is she?' Rees asked, his voice strained. His head felt as if a madman were swinging an axe round inside his skull.

'She didn't look nearly as bad as I'd expected, only there was a look in her eyes . . .' Timothy became silent.

'It'll take her a long, long time to come to terms with what happened,' said Christine. 'I don't suppose you or any other man can readily understand what it means.'

'We're beginning to have to learn,' said Rees. 'I read in the paper that another man has been raped in London.'

'God knows what kind of a world we're living in!'

'Probably not all that different; it's just that now we learn what's happening almost as it happens, whereas in the old days either it was kept hushed up or else not published until time blurred its impact.'

'If that's the case, I think I'd prefer to live then.'

'Only if you were healthy and wealthy.' Headaches made Rees quick to argue.

Timothy said: 'Calvin doesn't know about Penny.'

'Are you sure?' Christine asked.

'She told me he's not been to see her, so he can't do.'

'That's surprising.'

'What's the best way of telling him?'

'Come straight out with it,' Rees said. 'An oblique approach can often make things even more painful.'

Timothy returned to the hall. He braced his shoulders, picked up the receiver, dialled.

'This is Slade residence,' said Juan, the Filipino butler, making a mess of the 'th'.

'May I speak to Calvin, please?'

'Mr Calvin not home.'

He'd once joked about the pretentious way in which the butler had been taught to refer to Calvin; Calvin had not been amused. 'Has he gone to the hospital?'

'Not know, sir.'

'Is Mrs Slade at home?'

'Who calls?'

The other must have recognized his voice, but the procedure had to be adhered to. He gave his name, waited.

'Hullo, Tim.'

''Evening, Fenella.' She'd told him to call her by her Christian name; uncharitably, he'd thought that this was probably to make her feel closer to his age than her husband's. 'Sorry to bother you, but I wondered if Calvin's at the hospital?'

'When he left here, he said he was driving up to London.'

'He hasn't heard, then?'

'About Penny? I told him the moment he got back from the reunion.'

'You did? . . . Well, I just wanted to make certain he knows.' After replacing the receiver, he tried to make sense of what he'd just heard. Had he and Fenella been talking at cross purposes? It was inconceivable that Calvin could have known about the rape and yet not rushed to comfort Penelope. He checked the list of friends' telephone numbers, held in a small notebook, dialled the Slades' penthouse flat which overlooked Kensington Gardens.

'Yes?' Slade had no time for mere politeness.

'It's Tim speaking, Mr Slade. May I have a word with Calvin, please?'

The phone was put down without anything more being said.

'Hullo, me old cock,' said Calvin. 'What can I do for you?'

'I'm sorry, but I've some very bad news. Penny was attacked in her garden last night and the man . . . He raped her. She's in hospital.'

'Fenella told me.'

'But . . . but Penny says you haven't been to see her and so she thinks you don't know.'

'The fact is, hospitals give me the shits.'

'They're not my favourite place, but . . .'

'I've fixed up for flowers and some of her favourite truffles; they'll be delivered as soon as possible.'

'You don't think she might prefer you to flowers and chocolates?'

'Look, old man, as much as I want to be there, I just can't. It's like this. When I was a kid, I had acute appendicitis and was rushed into hospital without knowing what was going on. And when I came to after the operation I was in intensive care, wired up like a marionette. I was terrified and certain I'd been kidnapped by spacemen. Ever since, I haven't been able to go near a hospital.'

'Then you've made arrangements not to fall ill?'

'There's no call to be sarky. I was about to phone her and explain. She'll understand.'

'Then she's cleverer than I.'

'Hardly very difficult.'

'Would you by any chance like to hear how she is?'

'You sound like you've swallowed a pint of acid. Of course I bloody well want to know. I was just about to ask.'

'Physically, not too bad. But mentally, really suffering.'

'It's all very recent, of course.'

49

'What's your next priceless comment? Time heals.' He put the receiver down, returned to the sitting room.

The television was off and both his parents were reading. Christine looked up. 'How did he take it?'

He told them.

'How very extraordinary. I know what happens in childhood can be very traumatic and long lasting, but I'd have thought that by now he'd have come to terms with it.'

'Has he ever mentioned this appendix episode before?' Rees asked.

'No, why?' Timothy replied.

'Since he's very interested in himself, I'd have expected him to have related more than once and in great detail his struggle against the grim reaper.'

'What are you getting at?'

'The possibility that the history was a hurriedly thought up excuse.'

'If it's a load of bull, why didn't he rush to the hospital the moment he heard what happened?'

'Perhaps because he believes that Penny's partially or wholly to blame.'

Timothy stared at his father. 'Impossible.'

'That is being rather unkind,' Christine observed.

'In his case, I don't find that at all difficult.'

The morning was warm and sunny, the only clouds a few puffballs that wandered at the whim of the light breeze. Naylor braked the Ford Escort to a stop, climbed out on to the pavement, and walked along to number seventeen. He passed the wooden garage gates, came to a halt in front of the wrought iron garden gate. He inserted into the keyhole one end of the wrinkler he'd brought with him – a lock-examining tool which consisted of a very thin tube with a minute bulb, mirror, and lens, which enabled the interior of a lock to be visually examined. He peered down the tube, with the light switched on, battery in his left hand; he saw traces on the coat of oil, grease, and dirt that lay beyond the shiny parts where the key regularly touched. Those traces confirmed what he had assumed – the lock had been picked.

He opened the gate, walked up the flagstone path past an immaculate lawn – except where the rape and subsequent search had caused considerable disturbance – and weed free flowerbeds, nodded at the middle-aged gardener, stepped into the portico and rang the bell. Two days before, he would have envied the Hursts this large, comfortable house . . .

Diana opened the door and since he'd not met her before, he introduced himself. Her face was drawn and lined, her eyes reddened from recent crying; yet her manner was composed.

'You'd like a word with my husband?'

'And with you as well, if I may?'

'Come in.'

He followed her into the sitting room and she asked him to wait while she fetched her husband. Previously, he'd taken no note of the furniture and furnishings; now, with little else to do, he did so. The two Kirman carpets – not that he could have identified them – were filled with rich colour; the display cabinet contained a number of figurines which reminded him of some he'd recovered after a burglary and which had been said to be worth thousands; the strikingly patterned curtains were just what Hazel had wanted, but hadn't been able to afford . . . He stood as they entered.

'Good morning,' Hurst said. 'Please sit down.'

For him, their studied courtesy made their carefully suppressed distress that much more poignant. He sat, asked them how their daughter was.

'We returned from seeing her shortly before you arrived. Her injuries seem to be healing quite well.'

'I'm very glad . . . I'm sorry, but I'm going to have to ask you questions which may be distressing.'

'We understand. You may be assured that we shall answer them if we possibly can.'

Naylor had always been inclined to laugh at the do-my-duty-at-all-costs attitude, so often found in old wartime films; he did not find it humorous now. 'As I mentioned to you, Mr Hurst, I need a list of the names and addresses of your daughter's past boyfriends.'

'We have drawn one up.'

'That's great. You'll have thought a lot about this, so have you found any reason to believe that one of the men on the list could have been so insanely jealous that he might have attacked her?'

'Of course not.'

'It does happen.'

She said: 'As far as we know, each friendship ended quietly. I do remember that one of the boys was very upset, but he was far too nice to dream of attacking her.'

'I'd like you, nevertheless, to identify him when you give me the list . . . Your daughter never mentioned that one of her past friends was bothering her with phone calls, letters, that sort of thing?'

'No.'

'I understand she has a boyfriend now. What is his name?'

'Calvin Slade.'

'Would you imagine that he and your daughter have been having sex together?'

'Good God, man, what's that to do with you?' demanded Hurst violently. 'Do you gain some perverted pleasure . . .'

'Geoffrey!' His wife's voice was filled with pain, but firm.

'I have a very good reason for asking,' Naylor said quietly. 'If he was having sex with your daughter, it becomes almost certain that he cannot have been her attacker.'

She reached out and gripped her husband's hand. 'Some time ago, they were on holiday together. As much as we might prefer not to, we have to accept that in this day and age they did not sleep in different bedrooms.'

'Thank you, Mrs Hurst. Did your husband mention that I need your daughter's pants which, I believe, you found on the lawn?'

'They're upstairs.'

'Perhaps you'll let me have them at the same time as you give me the list of names . . . Although we have to check your daughter's past and present friends, the likelihood has to be that her attacker was either a complete stranger or, more probably, a partial stranger.'

'What the devil is a partial stranger?' asked Hurst roughly.

'Someone who knows her by sight, but whom she may never have consciously noted – the man behind a shop counter, in the ticket office at the railway station, that kind of person.'

'Why should her attacker more probably be someone like that?'

'Because of the circumstances. There were lights in the house, the garden gate was locked, and the time was after midnight. The obvious conclusion to draw from those facts would be that all the occupants of the house were at home for the night. Yet the assailant broke into the garden and waited there for quite some time which suggests he knew the house was empty. This raises the further possibility that he was certain your daughter would be returning on her own.'

'He couldn't have done.'

'Can you be quite certain of that? There was no one in this house on Saturday who might have overheard the arrangements being made?'

They looked at each other. 'The only people were the workmen,' she said.

'What workmen were they?'

'We've been having part of the house rewired. The firm said it would only take a couple of days, but there was always a reason why they couldn't have a full team here and it was obviously going to take considerably longer. I complained and so they worked on Saturday.'

'How many men were here then?'

'At one time there were three, but for most of the morning, only two.'

'Please think back and remember if you discussed what you were intending to do in front of any of them.'

After a while, she said: 'I had a word with Penny, just after she returned from the shops and one of the workmen came into the hall then.'

'What were you discussing?'

'I told her the Ashleys had rung and asked us all to dinner. She said she'd a previous appointment. So I said we could drop her at her friend's, but we couldn't pick her up because we'd be so late and she must get a taxi home because it would be so much safer than walking . . . Oh, my God!' Tears welled out of her eyes.

Naylor stared at the display cabinet and wished himself miles away.

'I'm sorry,' she said.

'Do you know the name of the electrician who was working in the hall?'

'I think I heard one of the others call him Rudolf.'

'And which firm does he work for?'

'Keen, Robinson.'

9

Grey lit his pipe, its bowl heavily charred, and puffed out clouds of acrid smoke. Naylor, standing in front of the desk, coughed. 'Are you recycling camel dung?'

'You're not paid to crack jokes that died years ago of old age . . . What's the report?'

'They gave me the pants and I've left them with Stores who'll get them to the lab. They also made out a list of past boyfriends.'

'Do any of them look promising?'

'The current one, Calvin Slade, is getting his oats, so we can forget him.'

'Slade? Anything to do with Franklin Manor?'

'That's his address.'

'Then we're moving amongst serious money. What about the others?'

'The parents named one who was really upset when the friendship broke up.'

'See he's questioned.'

'That's in hand. But much more interesting, Sarge, is the fact that on Saturday there were electricians in the house and Mrs Hurst remembers talking to her daughter in front of one of 'em and saying that she and her husband would be back after her and she was to get a taxi home. That could be promising.'

At first sight, the room seemed to be overflowing with cut flowers.

'One of the nurses said she's not seen anything like it

since Morwenna Evans was brought in with a broken ankle,' Penelope said.

'Who?' Timothy asked.

'Don't you read anything but the law reports? She's the actress who made such a hit in the revival of *Blithe Spirit* at the beginning of the year.'

She sounded, he thought, almost her normal, cheerful self. 'Presumably, the cornucopia is from Calvin?'

'Who else?'

'So where's the hundredweight of truffles?'

'Not quite that much, but enough that I daren't eat them all or I'll need an entire new wardrobe . . . How much longer are you going to stand there and not say hullo properly?'

As he leaned over and kissed her on the cheek, she gripped his right arm tightly and he realized that her recovery was not nearly as advanced as he'd first judged. After a moment, she released him. He straightened up, moved back and sat.

'Calvin phoned me this morning and created chaos because there's no socket in the room to take a phone. They had to find a phone with a really long lead. You'd have thought that in this day and age they'd have sorted that out. When he finally could get through, he said he'd have a mobile phone sent in so there wouldn't be any more trouble.'

'Chock full of initiative!' Initiative came more easily to those who could afford it.

'I told him it's not worth the effort since they're probably discharging me tomorrow.'

'They are? That's great.'

She began to fidget with the hem of the top sheet. 'They're suggesting I have more counselling.'

'You sound as if you don't think that's a good idea.'

'I told you what it was like last time. And even if they produce someone who doesn't remind me of my gym mistress, I don't . . . Well, I just don't want to talk about it.'

56

'Surely the whole idea is to get you to do just that because talking can help? It'll be with a professional stranger; rather like consulting a doctor.'

'You're always the sensible voice of reason, aren't you?' Her tone was bitter.

Was she remembering the past and wondering with regret why he'd so meekly stepped aside? . . . He cursed his mind for so unlikely, and untimely, a thought.

'As you're so sensible, explain something. Why hasn't Calvin been to see me?'

'But didn't he bring the flowers and truffles?'

'He had them delivered.'

'Oh! Then when he phoned you, didn't he explain?'

'He told me a story. I'm asking you for the truth. I needed him so desperately, but he never came.'

'When he was a kid . . .'

'He's not a kid now.'

'But what happens when young really can affect one for the rest of one's life. And it has a subjective influence, not an objective one, so it's impossible for someone else to . . .'

'Would you have stayed away as he has?'

'That's not a fair question.'

'Yes, it is, because you know that even if hospitals frightened you into the week after next, you'd still have come immediately you heard. What is it? Is he blaming me for letting it happen?'

'Of course he isn't.'

'I wonder,' she said bitterly.

Rodgers, a CID aide with G division, was not nearly as naïve as his wide, blue eyes and round, unlined face suggested. But if his youthful, innocent appearance was a liability when dealing with villains, it was an asset when he was questioning a protective mother.

'You're sure there's nothing wrong?' Mrs Richardson asked.

'Couldn't be more certain,' he replied. He was an efficient liar.

'Then I don't understand why you want to talk to him.'

'Because we've been asked to, by the other division. In a case like this, we have a word with anyone who might be able to help, however unlikely that is.'

'But Giles hasn't seen or spoken to her in a long time.'

'One never can tell. He might just have learned something then that'll help us catch the man now.'

'It's all so terrible.'

'It must have upset your son?'

'Of course it did. He was very fond of her and when their friendship came to an end . . . I always said it was her fault that he did so badly in the first year exams. At one point, it looked as if they wouldn't have him back. But we've an old family friend . . .'

'If I could have a word with him?'

She stood. 'I'll go up to his room and tell him you're here.' She left.

A clucking, over-protective mother, he thought. Which was in tune with lace curtains, twee furniture, arty knick-knacks, and the several framed photographs, one of which scaled the heights of schmaltz by featuring a crawling baby.

He had expected a willowy young man in horn-rimmed glasses who delighted in Shelley. Giles Richardson looked as if the only poetry he enjoyed was *The Miller's Tale*.

'You want a word with me about Penny?' he said, in a gravelly voice.

'That's right.'

'He says . . .' began his mother, who had followed him into the sitting room.

'That's OK, Mum.'

She hesitated, then left.

'How is she?' Richardson asked tightly.

'I'm sorry, but I can't answer. The other division didn't say.'

He balled his fists. 'What wouldn't I give for five minutes with the bastard!'

'Much better to leave us to deal with the matter.'

'Crap!'

Rodgers admired such belligerence. 'Can you remember when you last saw Miss Hurst?'

'The fifteenth of February, last year.'

A date obviously scored in his mind. 'Have you had any contact with her since then?'

'No.'

'Then you can't tell me anything about her recent life?'

'That's right, I can't.'

'Even so, can you suggest anyone who might have wanted to harm her?'

'No.'

'One last thing. Would you mind telling me where you were Saturday night?'

Richardson spoke with such violence that Rodgers automatically braced himself for an attack. 'You think I could have had anything to do with what happened? Then you're as goddamn sick as the bastard who did it.' He left the room, slamming the door behind himself.

Mrs Richardson looked into the room. 'Is something wrong? I thought I heard Giles shouting and then the door seemed to bang . . .'

'I'm afraid he's upset.'

'Oh, dear!'

'So upset, in fact, that he was about to tell me where he was Saturday night, but then his emotions got the better of him . . . To save making things worse for him, maybe you can tell me if he was at home?'

'Saturday evenings are the one time he takes off from his work. He does so need the break.'

'He went out?'

'With some friends.'

'I don't suppose you can say when he was back?'

59

'Just before midnight. I can never sleep until I know he's safe.'

WPC Carmichael said: 'Hullo, Miss Hurst. My word, it looks like a flower show!'

'Calvin has never done things by halves.'

He still hadn't visited her. Men could be such bastards. 'Is it all right if I sit?'

'Of course it is.'

'I've been on the go all day.'

'Would you like a truffle?'

'I can never say no to chocolate.'

'Help yourself.' Penelope indicated the very large, highly decorated box on the bedside table.

Carmichael helped herself to a truffle, bit it in half, ate. 'My word, I've not had anything like this before! Where are they from?'

'A shop in Jermyn Street imports them from Brussels.'

'Then I wouldn't mind a posting to Brussels!' She ate the second half, then wiped her lips with a handkerchief. 'They told me downstairs that you're going to be discharged tomorrow. I'll bet you're looking forward to that?'

'I . . .' Penelope stopped.

'Not too certain?'

'Mother suggests staying in a hotel for a while.'

'It's going to be tough, I'm afraid, whatever you do – there's no escaping that. But putting things off might not be the right answer. I'm no expert, but I have helped a number of women who've suffered what you have and I've seen how things turn out for them. Returning to where it happened is very frightening, but usually it has to be done sometime. Putting that moment off won't make it any easier and may even make it more difficult. I'd say, from talking to you, that you're a fighter. So fight; go straight back, walk into the garden, tell yourself, yes, happened there, but it's over and done with and it can't hurt your life any more.'

There was a long silence.

60

'I'm afraid there are more questions. Do you remember that there were some electricians working in your house on Saturday?'

'Yes.'

'Did you, by any chance, have cause particularly to notice one?'

'I don't think I understand.'

'Perhaps it seemed one of them was taking rather a lot of notice of you?'

'Are you suggesting that . . . that it was one of them?'

'Far from it. But we have to consider every possibility so that we can eliminate all those which obviously are nonsense.'

She thought for a while, her gaze unfocused. 'There was the man in the hall.'

'Tell me about him.'

'I'd just got back from the shops and Mother was talking to me and suddenly I had the impression that he was very interested in us.'

'Have you any idea why you thought that?'

'Not really, except that I'd noticed that although he looked as if he were working, he wasn't really doing anything. And it was he who earlier . . .'

'What happened earlier?'

'A couple of times when I went into the sitting room, I felt he was looking at me like . . . you know; as if he were mentally undressing me. I don't suppose that means anything. After all, it happens all the time.'

'At your age, it certainly does. Did he try to get friendly?'

'I don't think he ever actually spoke to me.'

'How would you describe him? Big, strong Michael Douglas type?'

'More like a shabby Woody Allen. And there was something about him that made me want to shiver. D'you know what I mean?'

'Exactly. Look, I know this is going to be hard on you, but I think you must tell me once more what happened, right from the beginning, in case you now remember something fresh. Quite often, a witness does. So start when the taxi turned into your road. Did you see any pedestrians? Was there a vehicle parked in front of your house?'

Penelope had read not long before that every woman who was raped was thrice raped; the first time when her body was violated, the second when she had to answer the police's questions, the third when, at the trial, she was vilified by the defence. She had suffered the first, was suffering the second . . .

Her voice strained, she remembered aloud until the moment before the rape took place.

'And then?'

'I've told you over and over, I can't remember any more.'

Carmichael recalled a previous rape case in the course of the investigation of which a doctor had said to her that the human mind was infinitely complex and infinitely individual. Where one remembered, another forgot; where one accepted, another rejected. Penelope had been so terrified and disgusted that her mind had pulled down a shutter to hide from her consciousness what was happening, as an anaesthetic protected a patient from pain. No amount of questioning would ever raise that shutter. 'When I last had a word with you, you talked about red poppies – have you any idea why they're significant?'

Penelope said, in a distant voice: 'In the spring, Calvin, Tim and I went for a walk. It was warm and sunny and there was a field that was covered with poppies. As I walked through them, I thought everything was so beautiful it was like a wonderful dream.'

Beauty had wiped out the ugliness; but it hadn't prevented its happening.

10

The office of Keen, Robinson was in Richmond Street; behind it lay a large brick built storeroom. The ferrety owner ran a successful business because he was suspicious by nature and trusted no one – some said that that even included himself.

'There's me and Florrie,' he said, nodding in the direction of the peroxide blonde who sat at a second desk.

A very personal secretary, Naylor thought uncharitably.

'I've seven lads on regular pay and another two I call on when I need 'em.'

'Who was working at Marchmont Road on Saturday?'

'Florrie!'

She pressed several keys on the work-board, read the screen of the VDU. 'Cahill some of the time, Burrell, and Oppenheim.'

'I'd like a word with them if that's all right by you?' Naylor said.

'Not if it's in working hours, it ain't.'

'Any particular reason why not?'

'Because their time has to be paid for.'

'Stick it on the next customer's bill, like always.'

'You blokes make me want to laugh.' He looked as if he would resist the impulse.

'Is there anyone around I can talk to now?'

'Florrie!'

She pushed her chair back, stood, walked across to the doorway at the back of the office and went through.

Well-oiled hips, Naylor thought. 'Would one of your chaps be called Rudolf?'

'Burrell.'

'Would you describe him as a good worker?'

'Wouldn't be here if he wasn't.'

Florrie returned. 'Sid's in for stores; he's just on his way out again.'

'I'll have a word with him before he leaves,' Naylor said quickly, before Nicholson could find a dozen reasons why that was impossible.

It was some ten minutes later, as Naylor asked Cahill a final question, that another man entered the storeroom through the doorway at the far end. Naylor, seated on a packing case, nodded. ''Morning. Who would you be?'

'What's it to you?'

'Local CID, making a few general inquiries.' He experienced a sudden sharp excitement. His statement had created momentary panic.

Burrell, quickly overcoming that panic, turned to Cahill. 'They're shouting for you at the job.'

'I can't be in two places at once.'

'You go along and keep 'em quiet,' said Naylor. 'And thanks for all your help, eh?'

Cahill collected a roll of wiring, left. Burrell went over to a row of open-ended lockers and brought out a box of insulated fasteners from one of them. He began to walk to the doorway.

'Hang on a minute.'

'What d'you want?'

'Just a quick chat. But first, you can introduce yourself.'

'Edward Burrell,' he answered surlily.

'Rudolf is a nickname?'

He didn't answer.

Sweating, Naylor thought. Penelope Hurst had said that the rapist had sweated as if a tap had been turned on. 'Were you working at Marchmont House on Saturday?'

'What if I was?'

'You must have heard what happened?'

64

'That was long after we'd left.'

'Don't get me wrong. I'm not suggesting for one moment you know anything about the attack on Miss Hurst. It's just maybe you saw something that'll help us. Like when you arrived or left, was there anyone in the road who was taking an interest in the house?'

'I didn't see no one.'

'No one in a parked car?'

'I've just said, ain't I?'

'You'll have to bear with me asking the same question time and again; it goes with the job. And when we see someone as badly hurt as Miss Hurst, it really makes us want to catch the bloke. A lovely girl, isn't she?'

'Can't say I noticed.'

'You're telling me you were in the house and didn't look? What are you in your spare time – a Trappist monk?'

'I had me work to do.'

'So you kept your head down? Sure avoids trouble, only it's difficult not to dream . . . Was any of your mates taken by her?'

'I wouldn't know.'

'You don't talk amongst yourselves?'

'I don't.'

'There's a lot of sense in that. What time did you leave the house?'

'One o'clock.'

'How did you get back here?'

'In the firm's van.'

'And then what happened?'

'Signed off and went home.'

'How?'

'On me bike.' He automatically looked to his right.

Naylor saw a large motorbike – he tentatively identified it as a Kawasaki – up on its rest in the corner of the shed. 'I know you've said, but after they've been asked before sometimes people remember. When you left in the van, did you notice anyone in the road who maybe looked a bit out of place or was acting strange?'

Burrell looked quickly at Naylor, then away. He sucked on his lower lip. 'It's funny you should say that.'

'It *has* made you remember?'

'There was this bloke on the other side of the road, leaning against a wall.'

'That's good. Did something make you notice him?'

'He was staring at number seventeen. Leastwise, he looked to be.'

'Very interesting.' And in complete contradiction to his earlier evidence. 'Can you describe him?'

'He was a big bloke and rough-looking.'

'How about some stronger details – height, build, colour of hair, shape of face, clothes?'

'He was too far away to tell much. I mean, being on the other side of the road and me not taking special notice of that sort of thing.'

'But you know he was rough-looking, so I'm guessing you observed more than you think you did. What was the colour of his hair?'

'I don't know nothing more than I've said.'

'Tell you what. When you're back home and enjoying a jar, try and picture him in your mind. And if you do remember something, make a note of what that is so as you can tell me another time.' Naylor slipped off the crate, stepped forward. He held out his arm, but kept his elbow into his side so that Burrell had to come close to shake his hand. 'Will you do that for me?'

'I won't remember nothing.'

'You never can tell, as the Eskimo said to the mermaid.' Naylor released his hand and stepped back; Burrell's breath reminded him of a sty that had not been cleaned out in months. 'Thanks for all your help. Greatly appreciated.'

He returned to the office, thanked Nicholson, winked at Florrie, left and walked down to the parked CID car.

The one-way system forced him to drive a semi-circle which took him past the marketplace, along Bank Street – the street of the forty thieves – and down Weymouth

Road. After parking at the back of the glass and concrete building, he took a lift up to the fifth floor.

He crossed the CID general room, nodding at Tyler, the only other occupant, picked up the phone from the next desk to his and, careful to keep the trailing lead free of snags, settled in his chair. He dialled home. 'Love, it's me. How's it going?'

'The little blighter's been trying to run the mile in three minutes.'

'What did they say at the clinic?'

'We ought to enter him for the two thousand and twelve Olympics . . . Everything's as it should be and no call for worry.'

'Thank God for that! I had to know, but we're up to our eyebrows in work so I'd better ring off. See you.' He replaced the receiver.

'It's far worse for the father,' Tyler said, 'but don't you ever tell her.'

'You think I'm that stupid? . . . Is the skipper in?'

'He was a quarter of an hour back.'

Naylor made his way along the corridor to the sergeant's room. Grey was working at a pile of forms. 'Sarge, I'm just back from Keen, Robinson. Rudolf turned up whilst I was there.'

Grey began to scrape the bowl of his pipe with the small blade of a penknife.

'His name's Edward; Rudolf is a nickname. When I told him I was CID, he was so rattled it sounded like castanets.'

'It happens with a lot of people.'

'He sweated.'

'Same comment.'

'The best is to come. First off, I questioned Sid Cahill and he told me that when they left the house, there definitely weren't any pedestrians in sight. Burrell started off by saying the same thing, then when I kept on at him, he suddenly remembered a rough bloke who seemed to be taking a lot of interest in number seventeen. Couldn't give any sort of a description.'

'He could judge he was rough-looking, though.'

'I put the same point to him.'

'With what result?'

'Just repeated himself. So then I shook hands, to get him close enough to smell his breath. Give me rotten eggs any day of the week.'

Grey put the knife down, tapped the bowl on the ashtray, filled it with tobacco. 'Did you ask him about Saturday night?' He struck a match, lit the pipe.

'No. I reckoned it was best to report in first.'

Grey puffed out clouds of smoke; the slight breeze coming in through the opened window lazily shredded them. 'What do you make of him?'

'A little rat of a man; looks as if he's been put together from spare parts. With his looks and breath, even the downmarket Toms'll fight shy of him. The only way he's going to get it is by rape. And that'll be doubly good because it'll make him feel strong and powerful.'

'The stereotyped picture of a rapist.'

'Which is why it's so often proved true . . . Sarge, it's all beginning to fit. The only way any outsider could have known the family would be out and the daughter would be first back on her own was by hearing 'em talk. Burrell was in the hall when Mrs Hurst told her daughter to take a taxi. Miss Hurst said he'd worried her because of the way he'd looked at her.'

'People have all sorts of premonitions – afterwards.'

'She said the rapist had foul breath. You can't get any fouler than Burrell's unless you fall in a cesspit.'

The pipe had gone out and Grey put it down on the ashtray. 'The Old Man's up at County HQ, but he'll be back later on. I'll have a word with him as soon as he's in.'

Metcalf had a long, thin, pointed face, light blue eyes that often became disconcertingly sharp, a Roman nose, a firm mouth and an equally firm chin. He was hard-working, enjoyed the unusual combination of being a good administrator and possessing an inquiring imagination, and had he not once betrayed himself as willing to break the rules if he thought this necessary (the Tyrell case had nearly broken him), his promotion to high rank would have been virtually assured.

He listened to Grey without once interrupting him, then said: 'We'll question him at his place.'

11

A market town, Southwold had hardly changed either in size or character from the end of the eighteenth century to the beginning of the twentieth. Then, a repair yard for railway rolling stock had been set up and this had encouraged other industry and soon the town had grown, eventually so changing its character that the market, previously in the centre, was banished to the outskirts. Industry had needed workers and so hundreds of terrace houses, unconcerned with the quality of life, had been built. Many of these had been demolished and replaced since the end of the Second World War, but many still remained; were it not for the parked cars, often new or nearly new, it would have been reasonable to suppose that only the very poor lived along such roads.

Metcalf knocked on the front door of number eleven, the paint of which was peeling. The door was opened. 'Mr Burrell. My name's Detective Inspector Metcalf, local CID, and this is DS Grey. Would it be convenient to have a word?' He possessed an ironic view of life and accepted Burrell's obvious consternation as evidence that either he was very guilty or very innocent.

'What d'you want?'

A flavour of Burrell's breath reached him. To suffer both rape and gassing . . . 'We think you may be able to help us?'

'I told the other copper, I don't know nothing.'

'You may think you don't, but there always has to be the chance that, in fact, you do. So we would like a chat.'

Reluctantly, Burrell stood to one side. They entered a small room that was dark, despite the late sunshine, in urgent need of decoration, shabbily furnished, and littered with rubbish. But the television set had a twenty-seven-inch screen and the hi-fi had cost a small fortune.

Metcalf sat on the settee, to the accompaniment of twanging springs. 'We're interested in the man you noticed when you were leaving Marchmont Road on Saturday.'

Burrell had regained a measure of composure, but beads of sweat were beginning to break out on his forehead. 'I couldn't see him well.'

'DC Naylor did mention that fact. But you've maybe remembered a little more about him. The slightest help you can give us could be very important.'

Burrell took this to mean that the unknown man had become their main suspect. 'I'll do what I can.'

'That's very good of you.'

Never buy a second-hand car from the DI, Grey thought.

'How tall would you say he was?' Metcalf asked.

'A bit more than me, I suppose,' Burrell answered.

'And at a guess, you're what — five eight, five nine? . . . So maybe he was six feet. Was he big in build?'

'Yeah. You know, plenty of meat on him.' Burrell was beginning to enjoy this chance of making fools of them.

'You called him rough, I think? Was that because of his clothes?'

'That's right.'

'So what was he wearing?'

'It looked like a dirty old T-shirt and jeans.'

'You were able to see it was dirty, then?'

Burrell said hurriedly: 'All I mean is, it kind of looked dirty. Only I can't be sure.'

'Of course not. But your impression is very useful. Had he a hat on?'

'No.' Over-confidence was not going to catch him out again. Describe a hat now and later he might be called upon to remember what he'd said . . .

'Was his hair at all unusual? Punk, or shaven, or anything like that?'

'No.'

'Was it styled?'

'It was just short back and sides.'

'And what sort of colour?'

'Light brown.'

'You're being very helpful,' Metcalf said, at his smoothest. Burrell was now sweating heavily and it was interesting that the description could have been of his own hair. 'Let's try for a broad outline of the face. What shape was it – round, oval, pear . . . ?'

It was fifteen minutes later when he said: 'I reckon that's about as far as you can take us. Which, frankly, is further than I'd hoped.'

Burrell was prompted into saying: 'When something diabolical happens, a bloke wants to do everything he can.'

'How I wish everyone was as citizen-minded.' Metcalf stood. 'All right, Jim?'

Grey was sufficiently surprised at being addressed by his Christian name almost to miss his cue, but just in time he said: 'There's one more thing, isn't there, sir?'

'There is? . . . Of course! Dammit, my memory's becoming as weak as a politician's promise.' He turned back. 'Just for the records, Mr Burrell, where were you Saturday night, say between ten and one in the morning?'

'I was with a couple of mates in their pad.'

'Would you be kind enough to give me their names and address?'

'Mike Fossen and Ned Daniels. They hang out in Thorndyke Street – forty-six.'

'That's fine. Once again, many thanks for your help.'

They left, returned to the car. Grey started the engine, waited for a bike to pass, drove out. 'He's our man!'

'And smart enough to have fixed up an alibi just in case.' All the evidence was circumstantial so far, but his years of service had taught Metcalf that while appearance was one of the worst guides to guilt, instinct was one of the best.

Something about Daniels worried a corner of Tyler's mind, but he could not pin down what or why. 'When did Burrell arrive here?'

'I dunno. About ten, I suppose.'

That matched Fossen's evidence. They did things together. 'And he stayed until when?'

'Until we all went to bed.' Daniels looked quickly at Tyler, then away. 'He slept downstairs, on the sofa.'

So even sewer rats had their limits. 'When did you split up?'

'Can't rightly say. May have been two.'

'Or eleven.'

'No way, man.'

'If you can't rightly say, you can't rightly be certain.'

'We was watching MTV until midnight and then the programme changed to a load of crap. So we played discs and had some more cans.'

'For two hours?'

'Could've been a bit less; could've been a bit more.'

'And Burrell was with you all that time?'

'That's what I've been saying.'

'You've been lying.'

'Me, man?'

'Lying harder than a dog scratches fleas.'

'I wouldn't lie to the likes of you.'

'I've a mind to knock the shit out of you to help you remember the truth.'

'You touch me, man, and I'm calling a mouthpiece.'

The world had gone that soft, Tyler thought scornfully. He left and drove back to the station. Halfway along George Street, a traffic snarl-up brought him to a halt and as he waited, he suddenly remembered why Daniels had teased his memory.

Grey was in his room. 'I've seen Fossen and Daniels,' Tyler said. 'They make a ripe couple.'

'Never mind their politics.'

'Their evidence matches. Burrell arrived at their place around ten and stayed there for the rest of the night. Though he slept downstairs in respectable solitude.'

Grey pushed away the folder immediately in front of him, sat back in the chair. 'Is it going to be difficult to break their story?'

'It's not going to be easy. Only there's one thing that might help. I came across Daniels some years back, when he was a young tearaway.'

'So he has a record. Is that really going to take us anywhere?'

'It might give us some pressure.'

'And it might not. You want to know the score? Unless Miss Hurst can start remembering, or we have some luck, we're struggling.'

Christine, standing by the side of Timothy at the window of the sitting room, said: 'Is there something wrong with the engine?'

Timothy grinned. 'Don't let him know you asked that – he paid vast sums of money for that exhaust music.'

They watched Calvin talking to an elderly pedestrian whose enthusiasm for the Bentley was obvious. Calvin used the hand throttle to rev up once more, then he pulled the mag switches to stop the engine.

'I love the leather strap over the bonnet and those dinky windscreens.'

'They're called aeroscreens.'

'A terrible waste, of course. On a par with giving Aunt Clara a glass of Château d'Yquem.'

'You're always hard on Calvin.'

'I find it impossible to respect someone who believes wealth brings privileges, but no responsibilities.'

'*Noblesse oblige* and all that jazz?'

'I know your generation laughs at such a concept, but that merely shows how standards have dropped.'

'I'll bet your parents had the same moan.'

'Defend him as hard as you like, I have my opinion.'

'Which wild horses won't shift.' Certainly, her opinion would even have hardened had she known why Calvin was there. Moral cowardice would have been her kindest expression.

She turned away from the window. 'If he'd like coffee, let me know; I'll be in the kitchen. And that reminds me, lunch won't be until one-thirty because Nick won't be back until then.'

'Is he hoping finally to secure that work?'

'Fingers crossed.'

As she left the room, moving with a brisk grace that was a legacy of her keen interest in athletics when young, he wondered just how critical it was that his father secured the work he was hoping to be given? Finance was tight, but that was normal; was it, though, much tighter than he suspected? It was the one subject on which his parents never spoke frankly to him because they were afraid that he might give up reading for his degree and seek a job immediately in order to ease their financial burden.

He watched the old man pat the bonnet of the Bentley with the same respectful affection with which he would have patted the flanks of his favourite hunter, then walked on. Calvin crossed the pavement.

Timothy went through to the hall and opened the front door. 'Mother's offering coffee.'

'I had some at home. Let's go.'

His mother would certainly have noticed that lack of a 'thank you'.

He had expected it to be a reunion which he found embarrassing, without being able to define exactly why. He discovered that instinct had served him true. Penelope sought the reassurance of unaltered affection, Calvin would – or could – not give this. In consequence, they used him as a buffer. He was grateful when Diana came into the sitting room and said: 'I'm sorry, Penny, but the police are here and want to talk to you.'

'Not again?'

'I tried to push them off, but they say it's very important. I know it's hell, but if you don't see them now, they'll just come back another time.'

'Then I suppose I'll have to see them.' She reached across the settee to grip Calvin's hand.

Diana left, to return almost immediately with WPC Carmichael and Grey.

Carmichael said: 'It's great to see you back home, Miss Hurst. How are things?'

'Getting better.'

But only very slowly, Carmichael thought. Nightmares, deep depressions, constant fear, even self-hatred? Relationships could change, bewildering and causing, or adding to, a sense of guilt . . . 'This is Detective Sergeant Grey. I can't remember whether you've met before?'

'I've not had the pleasure,' said Grey, with old-fashioned courtesy. 'I'm very sorry to have to bother you like this, but there's something I want to show you.' He spoke to Calvin and Timothy. 'If you gentlemen wouldn't mind, I think it will be best if we speak to Miss Hurst on her own.'

Timothy expected Calvin to argue, as always arrogantly challenging authority. He was surprised when Calvin released Penelope's hand and stood.

'You won't leave?' she said, her expression one of pleading.

He looked at his wristwatch.

'Please, please.'

'No, I won't.'

After they'd left the room, Grey said: 'I'd like you to look at a photograph.'

'Of whom?'

'A man.'

'The one who . . . attacked me?'

'That is what we hope to find out.' He brought a photograph from his pocket and handed it to her.

Carmichael unobtrusively moved closer, ready to give

76

what comfort she could if the photograph provoked a hysterical reaction. She was not really surprised when Penelope remained outwardly calm.

'His face is blacked out.'

'Your attacker was wearing a hood. What I'm really asking now is if the build of the man in the photo is similar to the build of your attacker?' Would she realize from this how thin was the evidence at the moment, Grey wondered.

'I didn't see him until he'd forced me to the ground and then he seemed so terribly tall . . . I've told you all this before.'

'We're hoping you'll notice something about the man in the photo that seems familiar.'

Penelope studied the photograph again. 'He looks . . . Well, as if he doesn't fit together too well.'

The photograph had been taken from inside an unmarked van that had been parked outside the office of Keen, Robinson. Burrell was in mid-stride and his stance emphasized the awkwardness of his body.

'Would you describe your attacker as clumsily built, in the way that the man in the photo is?'

'The man who was in the hall on Saturday looked ungainly. I can remember thinking that his neck didn't seem to fit. He heard Mother and me talking about my catching a taxi home. And I saw him looking more than once as if he were nastily interested. That's who it is, isn't it?'

'I can neither confirm nor deny that. But please remember, Miss Hurst, that in the course of most investigations there are several possible suspects and it's as much our job to eliminate those who are completely innocent as to identify whoever's guilty.'

'How would my telling you that my attacker's build was like this man's eliminate him as a suspect?'

'That's not what I was saying.'

'Isn't it?'

'We don't need to bother you any more, Miss Hurst.

Perhaps I could have the photo back?' He should, he thought, as he stepped forward and held out his hand, have realized that however much she had suffered and was suffering, nothing had happened to impair her intelligence.

Penelope said: 'It was that electrician.'

'You can't be certain,' protested Timothy. 'Not with the face blacked out.'

'Why won't you believe me?' she demanded shrilly.

'They didn't actually identify him . . .'

'Because they're like you, so bloody cautious they have to look in a mirror to confirm they're still alive.'

'That bastard's going to rot in jail,' Calvin said, with vicious anger.

12

He introduced himself as he stood inside the porch. 'Detective Constable Naylor, local CID.'

'Good morning,' she said.

She'd be a dab hand at passing the cucumber sandwiches. 'I'm sorry to bother you, but I'd be grateful for a word.'

'Perhaps you'd like to come inside?'

He stepped into a hall that was furnished in best suburban style, right down to the cut glass vase full of flowers arranged à la Constance Spry.

'I suppose you're here because of that terrible thing which happened on Saturday night?'

He imagined that she found it difficult to speak the word 'rape'. 'We're talking to everyone in this road and the next two to discover if anyone can help us.'

'I don't see how I possibly can, but I certainly wish I could. It's all so very frightening.'

'There's no call to be afraid since we'll soon arrest the man, Mrs . . . ?'

'Fanshaw. Without an E.'

The name suited her, right down to the absent E. 'How you can help, Mrs Fanshaw, is by saying whether or not you were in all that evening.'

'Why should that matter?'

'It's like this. When someone sets out to commit a crime, any crime, he usually has a look at the target to make certain everything's smooth. So the odds are that the rapist didn't go straight to number seventeen, but first made sure the coast was clear. In doing that, he may well have drawn attention to himself.'

'I don't understand how.'

'By trying so hard to be inconspicuous that he became conspicuous.'

'I see,' she said doubtfully.

'So if anyone in this house was outside between ten and half past midnight on Saturday, they might have noticed him without realizing why ... Would anyone from here have been?'

'As a matter of fact, we had dinner with friends and drove back early because my husband had to get up at seven the next morning for his golf. We arrived here soon after ten.'

'So who was around – were there any pedestrians?'

'I certainly don't remember seeing any.'

The rapist would have known that there would be few people on foot at night in a neighbourhood where each house boasted a his and a her car and quite often a their car in addition. 'What about vehicles?'

'There were a couple of cars ahead of us.'

'Did you recognize either of them?'

'My husband said that one of them was the Stevens'; I can't say I would know whether it was or wasn't.'

'And the other?'

'I've no idea whose it was.'

'Were there any vans or motorbikes?'

'I don't ...' She stopped, frowned. 'Now I come to think about it, soon after turning into the road, we did pass a motorbike that was going very slowly. My husband remarked how unusual it was to see a big, powerful bike being driven so slowly.'

'I don't suppose you've any idea what make it was?'

'A Kawasaki,' she answered, a trace of triumph in her voice.

'Can you be certain?'

'You think I'm making it up?'

'Perish the thought, Mrs Fanshaw. It's just that most

ladies don't know one bike from another and it's so great to meet one that does.'

His apologetic explanation mollified her. 'I've been very interested in them from the days when my younger brother bought one against the wishes of my parents. He often took me for rides and I found that very exhilarating.'

He decided that he'd misjudged her; pure suburbia now, maybe, but once upon a time . . . 'Can you go on to say what model it was?'

'I'm afraid my interest isn't that detailed.'

'Was it a new bike?'

'All I can say is, it was in very good condition.'

'What colour?'

'Either white or cream.'

'Could you see anything of the rider's face?'

'He had on an all-enveloping helmet with a heavily tinted visor – the kind that make people look threatening because one can't see their eyes. Eyes are a great indicator of character, aren't they?'

'I've always found them to be,' he replied, although the sweetest pair of eyes he'd met had been those of a woman who had three-parts killed a man. 'What colour was the helmet?'

She thought for quite some time. 'Probably red; but, of course, it's difficult to be certain in street lighting.'

'Did it have any pattern on it?'

'There was some sort of a square, in colours.'

'How large?'

'Probably no more than two or three inches; I should think it was a kind of sticker.'

'I don't suppose you noticed the registration number?'

She shook her head.

'Not even the year letter?'

'I'm sorry. Would that have helped?'

'It could have done,' he replied.

When Naylor entered the office of Keen, Robinson, only Florrie was present. 'So where's the boss?'

81

'Out on the job.'

He grinned broadly. 'There's a lucky man, able to mix pleasure with business.'

She said sharply: 'On the job of work. Do you want something?'

Before his marriage he might well have been tempted; he'd always found thick, curling lips to be an infallible sign. 'I'm wondering which of the lads is out back?'

'As far as I know, no one. We've a big job for the council.'

'But Rudolf might have slipped back for a packet of screws, so would you have any objection if I go through to find out?'

'Why are you so interested in him?'

'He's helped us already and I'm hoping he'll be able to help us a whole lot more. Nice bloke. Good at his job, is he?'

'Like Mr Nicholson told you, he wouldn't be working here if he wasn't.'

'Pity about his breath. I suppose no one's ever told him about it?'

'The other lads never stop.'

'Must slow down his love life.'

'How should I know?'

'A good question . . . I'll just slip through and find out if by any chance he's there, then.'

He went through the doorway and into the long shed. The white Kawasaki, up on its rest, was in the same place as before. The registration number marked it as many years old, but it had been resprayed, the chrome work was undimmed, the tyres virtually unworn, and it could easily have been almost new. There was no helmet on the saddle or hung on a handlebar. He looked round and immediately saw a helmet in one of the open compartments nearby. Medium to dark red, a heavily tinted visor, and on either side a multi-coloured, square decal proclaiming the Z1000 to be the bike of the century.

*   *   *

Grey looked across his desk. 'Sure, it fits neatly. But as evidence, it's nothing.'

'Come off it, Sarge. OK, it's not all that strong . . .'

'She can identify a Kawasaki, but not the model or the year and she's no idea of the registration number. The rider's helmet was probably red, but she can't be certain; there was something on the side of it which might have been a decal, but then again, might not.'

'Each point on its own may not mean much, but add them all together . . .'

'And a judge would still make a dog's dinner of the prosecution's claim that Mrs Fanshaw's evidence proves Burrell was in Marchmont Road just after ten.'

'If only the old girl had noticed the registration number.'

'Miracles stopped with the coming of Coca Cola. And for that much, even if she'd identified it as Burrell's bike, how would that prove he was in the garden of number seventeen at twelve-thirty?'

'The dumbest jury would have to draw that conclusion.'

'You've a sight more confidence in juries than I have . . . For the moment, we'll accept that it was Burrell, sussing out the area. What would he do once he was satisfied all was quiet?'

'Find somewhere to park the bike where it wouldn't readily be connected with the rape, but would be handy enough for a smart getaway.'

'So start looking for that somewhere.'

Fossen possessed all the charm of a dropsical hyena. 'I told the other bloke.'

'And now you're going to tell me.' Tyler stared at the empty beer cans on the floor and wondered how anyone could choose to live amidst such slovenly disorder. 'When did he arrive here?'

'Somewhere around ten.'

'Try again.'

'Around ten.'

'You know something? I've questioned more villains

than I can count on a pocket calculator, yet I still haven't learned why someone can be stupid enough to go on lying when that makes him look a bloody fool. Just after ten, he was sussing out Marchmont Road on his bike.'

'Not Rudy.'

'And soon after that, he parked his bike and walked to number seventeen, picked the lock of the gate, let himself into the garden, and waited. At half past twelve, the daughter stepped into the garden, he put a knife to her throat and then he raped her.'

'He was here. We was watching MTV until midnight and when the programme changed . . .'

'What did it change to?'

'I . . . I don't remember.'

'Of course you don't remember because Rudy wasn't here and you weren't watching the telly.'

'You can ask Ned.'

'And remind him that with his form, it doesn't do to get us so annoyed we start feeling nasty. So before he turns you into a liar who's done his best to pervert the course of justice, let's have the truth so we'll remain friendly.'

'He was here all night after ten.'

13

Timothy opened the gate, stepped into the garden, and automatically looked to his left. Would time and her own inner strength help Penelope to escape her memories?

The front door was opened by Diana. She looked beyond him, then said: 'No Calvin?'

'He's very sorry, but he couldn't make it.'

'Come on in.'

He stepped inside, closed the door. 'How is Penny?'

'I think, a little more cheerful . . . Tim, will you give me a couple of minutes before you go through and see her?' Without waiting for an answer, she led the way past the sitting room to the study, in which the books on the shelves testified to the family's wide range of interests. 'I'm hoping you'll do me a favour.'

'If I can, I will,' he answered, uneasily certain what he was about to be asked.

'Is Calvin deliberately staying away?'

'I suppose that in one sense he is; but in another, he isn't.'

'Can you explain what you mean?'

He wasn't sure he could. 'When he was young, he had to be rushed into hospital . . .'

'I know all about that and, frankly, I don't believe a word of it. Suppose it had been you, would you have stayed away from Penny now?'

'I don't think that's really a very fair question.'

'Why not?'

'Because a person's response to a situation has to be completely subjective.'

'Are you saying you would have stayed away if you were as scared of hospitals as he claims to be? Nonsense. You'd have very quickly forced yourself to overcome that fear. So why hasn't he?'

He made no answer.

'And if it was a fear of hospitals, why didn't he come here the moment Penny returned home, instead of waiting until you were with him? . . . I'm sorry, Tim, I know I'm putting you in an impossible position because you and he are friends. But it's so distressing to see how bewildered Penny is because of the way he's acting.' She stared into space. 'I've read that there are men who turn their backs on wives or girlfriends who've been raped. I've never believed that a decent man could do such a thing; I've been certain he'd do everything in his power to comfort her and help her overcome the horrific experience. Is Calvin blaming her for what happened?'

'That's impossible.'

'Are you so sure he hasn't convinced himself she encouraged the swine so that in his mind he can justify his own reactions?'

'He knows she'd never have done that.'

'It's not a question of what he knows, but of what he wants to know.'

'But why?'

'Because he sees her rape as an insult to him.'

'No.'

'You're a very loyal friend. Would that he was . . . Please don't tell Penny about this conversation. And one last thing. I'm trying to persuade her to go to the States for a complete change. I expect she'll ask you for your opinion. Your approval will carry a lot of weight, so will you say you think it's a wonderful idea?'

'Yes, of course.'

She stepped forward and briefly touched his arm. 'Thanks for everything.'

Penelope had taken trouble with her appearance and was wearing one of the most colourful of her print frocks; she looked far more her old self. As he entered the sitting room, she switched off the video and television. 'What a great alternative to a really boring film!'

He grinned. 'If it was that boring, the alternative doesn't have to be very hot!' He crossed to the settee, kissed her on both cheeks, moved back to a chair and sat.

'You're doubly welcome because I need some advice.'

'Presumably, boringly cautious, stick-in-the-mud advice?'

'What else? Mother's been on and on at me, saying I need a complete break and should go to Florida to stay with Aunt Kelly. What do you think of the idea?'

'Pack.'

'It's not like you to be so definite, so quickly. Mother must have nobbled you before you came in here and asked you to say that?'

'No way.'

'Your ears are waggling, which means you're lying. Forget what she said and tell me what you really, honestly think.'

'What reason is there for not going?'

'Because I so want to go.'

'Can you get more Irish than that?'

'Don't you understand? The inner voice keeps telling me I long to go because I want to escape.'

'Escape what?'

'Don't you remember the policewoman telling me . . . No, you wouldn't, because you weren't there.'

'At long last, a hint of logic!'

'Stop being facetious, this is really important. She told me it would be tough; that when I went into the garden, I'd look at where it happened and my mind would be knifed; that until the man was caught, I'd be scared of shadows. And the only real way of overcoming the fear was to meet it head on; to step into the garden and deliberately stare at where it happened and tell myself the bastard will never attack me a second time. But if I go to Florida, I'll be running away from the fight.'

'Only after you've won it.'

She spoke in wondering tones as she stared at him. 'You really think I can have won it after only five days? You're much too understanding to begin to believe that. You're not being honest and are trying to persuade me to do what Mother wants.'

'She doesn't come into it. You *have* won the first fight. You couldn't be talking like this if you hadn't. And it's the first one that the policewoman meant. Sure, there'll be black days. But have a complete break in the States and you'll build up mental strength and be ten times better able to meet them when they come.'

'You sound like a PR man on full throttle.'

'I'm sorry. But . . .'

'For Christ's sake, stop apologizing.'

'All right. If you don't go, you'll be stupid. That is, unless you don't get on with your aunt.'

'I think she's fabulous because she's the joker of the family. She's been divorced twice and from her last letter, divorce number three is waiting in the wings. The trouble is, she can't stand being serious and Americans become so very serious over money. Four years ago, Mother sent her an invitation to their wedding anniversary purely as a memento; she took the first plane, arrived totally unexpectedly, stayed one night, and returned the next day. Husband number two worked out what that had cost and grew another ulcer.'

'She sounds exactly the right tonic for you.'

'Then will you make it a double-action tonic and come with me?'

'I would if I could, but there's not a chance.'

'The ticket would be a present.'

'Thanks, but it's still no.'

'I was afraid you'd be like this.' She was silent for a while and her expression became bitter. 'Will you promise me something? When they catch the man, there'll be the trial and I'll have to go into the witness box and say what happened. The mackintosh brigade will be licking their lips, and God knows what else, and it'll be revolting. So promise me you'll be in court so that when things get too horrible I can look across and see you.'

'I'll be there.'

As Naylor left the CID Escort, Grey came out of the building and crossed the car park to his somewhat battered Rover. Naylor hurried over.

Grey, his hand on the opened driving door, said: 'If it won't keep until tomorrow, make it really short. I'm due home three-quarters of an hour ago.'

'No one noticed a parked Kawasaki Saturday night.'

'That could have waited.'

'Was there any joy with Fossen?'

'He's sticking like superglue to his story. Unless Forensic come up with something good, this case is heading for the deep freeze.'

'Someone must have seen Burrell arrive at Thorndyke Street on his bike on Sunday morning.'

'I've had three lads out all day, asking. It seems the whole bloody neighbourhood was tucked up in bed, asleep, like the good, honest citizens they claim to be.'

'Why don't we go in and search Burrell's place?'

'Because we'd have to stretch the evidence to breaking point to persuade a magistrate to sign the warrant.'

'So stretch it.'

'Haven't you yet learned the one golden rule? Never put your own nuts on the block, only other people's?'

'Can I speak to Calvin, please?' Timothy said over the phone.

'I tell Mr Calvin.'

He waited.

''Evening, old man. How's the world?'

'I'm just back from seeing Penny; she's a lot brighter.' He waited for some comment; there was none. 'Her mother's suggested a clean break and that she flies to the States to stay with her aunt.'

'Sounds a good idea.'

'It seems she'd like some support, at least to begin with. So I wondered if you'd fly with her?'

'Love to, but no can do. The old man's in one of his difficult periods and keeps moaning it's time I worked myself into the business instead of enjoying life. When he's like that, the only thing to do is swing along with him until he finds something else to worry about.'

'Then make certain you see her before she leaves.'

'Who the bloody hell appointed you my mentor?'

The sudden, rough anger surprised Timothy. Later, and on reflection, he decided that it should not have done so.

Forensic phoned on Monday. All the samples proved to have come from the victim; the attempt to raise finger-prints on her pants had failed.

Grey went through to the DI's room and was writing out a résumé of the call when Metcalf hurried in. 'Yes?'

'Just leaving a note to say Forensic have come through in the Hurst case. No joy.'

Metcalf sat, stared at Grey for several seconds, then said: 'We'll search his place.' Unlike the other, he was prepared to take risks.

The search team was led by Metcalf.

'You ain't coming in,' said Burrell.

Metcalf, hopefully out of smelling distance, handed him the warrant.

'You won't find nothing.'

An hour and a quarter later, they had to agree. His shoes were size ten, but none were of the right pattern or had earth or grass on the soles; he had several pairs of jeans and trousers, but none held traces, even when viewed under the portable ultraviolet light; there were two long woollen scarves but his jeering smile told them, as they packed these into plastic bags to take away, that neither had been used in the rape; they found no masks of any kind, condoms, or pornographic magazines or tapes.

As they drove away, Metcalf said bitterly: 'Burned what he was wearing and chucked out anything else that might have fingered him.'

Metcalf looked across his desk at Naylor and Grey. 'We're going to have to put the case into cold storage. All the while Burrell has that alibi, we're wasting our time.'

'Why don't we put real pressure on Fossen and Daniels?' Naylor asked.

'We've gone as far as we can.'

Naylor knew Grey was willing him to shut up, but he said: 'They're probably busy. If we found out their line of country, we could do a spot of horse trading.'

'That could take weeks. Even at the end, there could be no guarantee that any threat from us would be strong enough.'

'Then let's broaden the search for someone who saw his parked Kawasaki.'

'Where's the guarantee that anyone did?' Metcalf stood, walked over to the window and looked out. 'We're strapped for hands as it is and I'm left to decide priorities. With a dozen and one hot cases, one that's gone cold loses all priority after a certain period. In my judgement, the Hurst case has reached that point.'

'But . . .'

He swung round and stared at Naylor. 'Goddamnit, do you think I like making the decision any more than you like hearing it?'

14

On Thursday, the ever-changeable weather brought blue skies and the lightest of breezes. Christine stood in the doorway and the lower half of her was in sunshine. She waited for Timothy to walk up the path, then said: 'Penny phoned from Heathrow just after you'd left.'

'She's on her way to Florida? Must have made her mind up and found a flight in double-quick time.'

'I have an idea that the family knows someone with pull. She was very sorry to miss you and was going to ring again just before boarding, but I said you probably wouldn't be back. She'll be in touch after she arrives. She sounded quite cheerful.'

'When I saw her yesterday, she was a lot better.'

'She's courageous. With all her strengths, I've never understood why she's so friendly with Calvin.'

'Perhaps you would if you weren't so prejudiced.'

'How can I be any less prejudiced when he's so beastly to her?'

'Your dislike goes back long before this trouble.'

'But is exacerbated by it. I suppose you realize that he views Penny's rape as much more of a tragedy for himself than for her?'

'Come off it.'

'She's betrayed him by becoming damaged goods.'

'That's a filthy thing to say.'

'Where he's concerned, I could talk a lot filthier.' She turned abruptly, hurried through to the kitchen.

He entered and shut the door. His mother, like Diana

Hurst, was judging events objectively. Perhaps for women, rape was so shocking none could judge subjectively.

Timothy was on his own when he heard a familiar, bellowing roar. He crossed to the window and watched Calvin climb over the side of the Bentley on to the running board and then down on to the pavement. He remembered his mother's comment that such a car in Calvin's hands was a pearl cast before swine.

He went through to the hall, opened the door. 'Penny's flown off to the States.'

'I know.' Calvin stepped inside.

'You saw her off?'

'I saw her last night, but she only told me what was happening when I rang this morning to cancel lunch . . . I need a stiff drink. If you haven't the necessary, I've emergency supplies in the tool box.'

'We may not have too much Krug in the cellar, but we've something in the larder. Come on through.'

In the sitting room, Calvin slumped down in one of the chairs.

'What would you like – gin, whisky, Cinzano, or lager?'

'Whisky. With ginger if you've got that.'

Timothy went through to the larder, poured out a whisky and ginger and a gin and tonic, carried the glasses through, handed one to Calvin. He sat.

'Penny was in a hell of a state,' Calvin said.

'She was? When I saw her earlier, she seemed a lot more cheerful. But I suppose she's bound to suffer sharp swings of mood.'

'You know what's really getting her down, don't you? It's the knowledge that that bastard is still free, even though the police know he raped her. It makes her feel betrayed as well as frightened.'

'It's easy to understand. But until the police can gather sufficient evidence . . .'

'What if they never do?'

'Then they'll never make an arrest.'

'So you don't give zilch that Penny's going to go on and on feeling terrified and betrayed because she knows he's still free?'

'I care one hell of a lot. But the law says . . .'

'And rules and regulations are infinitely more important than Penny's future happiness?'

'It's hell when something like this happens to someone one knows, but the law . . .'

'And I always thought you really liked her!'

'You know damned well I do.'

'But only when the going's smooth. Which makes me all kinds of a fool for expecting you'd join in.'

'Join in what?'

'Making certain the bastard is put behind bars so that Penny can stop feeling frightened and betrayed.'

'That's out of our reach. Only the police can do that.'

'I've news for you. They're dropping the case.'

'That's impossible.'

'Dad has contacts and I've talked to one of 'em. The police can't break the alibi. So they're giving up Penny's case and concentrating on cases they can solve because that makes for good publicity.'

'I don't believe it.'

'Happens all the time. And especially when they're dealing with someone in Penny's situation.'

'What are you suggesting now?'

'Isn't it obvious? She comes from a reasonably well-off home.'

'What difference does that make?'

'The police are paid peanuts, so when someone very much better off meets trouble, they're not going to work themselves to death on her behalf since they reckon that it's only fair she should suffer hassle.'

'That's crap!'

'Then why is the detective in charge so quick to call a halt to the investigation? . . . It's no good sitting back and believing the police are doing anything. If it's left to them, the bastard rapist is going to stay free.'

'But . . . but if they really are closing the investigation, there's nothing anyone else can do.'

'Dead wrong. We make certain the bastard's brought to trial.'

'How?'

'Before I answer that, are you with me?'

There was a long silence.

'Forget it,' Calvin said contemptuously. He drained his glass, stood. 'I'll make it a solo job.'

'If . . .'

'You're full of brave words on Penny's behalf until it's a case of actually doing something. Then you can think up a dozen reasons for leaving her to suffer hell.'

'What . . . what are you going to do?'

'Isn't it obvious? The police know it was the electrician, but claim they can't arrest him because of an alibi. I'm going to persuade the bastard to admit that his alibi is false.'

'By bribing him?'

'You think he'd open his mouth for cash when to do so would mean he'd head straight for jail?'

'The only alternative is force. And I don't give a damn what you say or think, I won't have anything to do with that. In any case, if force were used, his confession would be inadmissible in court.'

'What it is to have a lawyer by one's side! I don't use force, Mr Rees, QC, I use the threat of force. That way, there's nothing he can do to prove that the confession should be inadmissible.'

'What kind of threat?'

'The Elejumper.'

'Which is what?'

'A gadget from the States, based on the electrical cattle prod, that women carry in their handbags to protect themselves. The Old Man brought one back for Fenella, but she never carries it around with her; I think she read it was illegal over here. After I've explained to that bastard what it feels like to have an Elejumper applied to his more

95

delicate parts once they've been doused in water, he'll be ready to admit he's Jack the Ripper.'

'When the police learn he's been threatened . . .'

'With not a mark on him, it's not going to be easy to convince them there's as much as a shadow of truth in his story. And even if he could succeed in that, he won't be able to identify me since I'll be wearing a ski-mask.'

'You'll be the prime suspect.'

'But I've learned how things work. The police can be certain you're guilty, but if you've an alibi, they have to whistle. I'll have an alibi they'll never break.'

'Who'll give you that?'

'Fenella.'

'Why should she take the risk?'

'Because she's got used to a Ritz life and would hate like hell to go back to where she was. But my old man dropped my mother for her and so she's always wary in case he does the same to her for some bimbo. Which means that she takes great care to be nice to me so that I don't start suggesting to the Old Man that he made a bit of a mistake . . . But what's all that to you? Or are you finally beginning to think of Penny rather than yourself?'

'I'm with you,' Timothy said hoarsely.

15

'I'm having a meal with Calvin and after that we're going out somewhere so I'll probably be back late,' Timothy said.

'All right, dear. I'll leave you to have a lie-in in the morning.' Christine studied him over the top of the book she had been reading.

'What's the matter?'

'I was wondering if something's wrong.'

'Why should it be?'

'If I knew the answer, I wouldn't be wondering.'

He hesitated, then said: 'The pressure of work is beginning to bite.'

'And how many times have I suggested you don't go at it quite so hard? Anyway, for one night at least, forget all about torts and contracts and have real fun. Do you need some money?'

'No, thanks.'

'I wish . . .' She cut the words short.

He knew what she'd been going to say – 'I wish you'd stop accepting so much from Calvin.' This time, though she was not to know, he was accepting nothing.

'What about transport?'

'He's picking me up.'

'In the Bentley?'

'I imagine so.'

'I'd have thought by now he'd have got fed up with that and exchanged it for something more in tune with his character.'

'Presumably, you'd suggest a stretched Cadillac limo with smoked windows?'

Calvin brought the thudding Bentley to a halt in front of tall tubular and wire mesh gates, across the top of which ran three strands of razor-wire. 'Here's the key of the padlock.' He passed it across.

'What is this place?'

'A coldstore belonging to one of the old man's companies.'

Timothy opened the tiny passenger door, stepped on to the vibrating running board and down on to the road. He crossed to the gates, unlocked the padlock, slipped the chain free, pushed the gates open. Tension was knotting his stomach, drying his mouth, and making his heart seemingly beat at many times its normal rate.

Calvin drove the Bentley through and parked it against the wall of the nearest building. He undid the tonneau cover over the back seats, picked up a cardboard box and put this on the running board, opened it.

'What's that?' Timothy demanded as he stared down at a snub-nosed automatic.

'Exactly what it looks like.' Calvin's voice was strained; his sang-froid was assumed, his sense of tension every bit as great as Timothy's.

'For God's sake, we can't take that.'

'How else do we make certain he doesn't shout his head off before we gag him?'

'If we're armed, we're committing a far more serious offence.'

'Since no one will be able to pin anything on us, so what?'

'Is it loaded?'

'No.'

'Are you sure?'

'Pull the magazine out and find out for yourself.'

It was empty.

'Don't forget to make certain there isn't one up the spout,' Calvin said with heavy sarcasm.

He did so.

'Finally satisfied?'

He was satisfied he was a complete, bloody fool to have let himself be drawn into this stupidity.

They donned blue ski-suits.

'You hang on here,' Calvin said, 'while I get a key to one of the vans.'

He waited in the shadow of the building, desperately wishing himself anywhere but where he was.

Calvin returned. 'Come on.'

There were five refrigerated vans lined up in a long lean-to, at the back of the first building. The tab on the key identified the end van and Calvin unlocked the offside door, slid it back, settled behind the wheel after releasing the lock of the nearside door. As Timothy sat, he started the engine.

As they neared the gates, Timothy suddenly realized that these had been left open instead of having been closed behind them. It had only needed a patrolling police car and they could have been caught red handed. They were rank amateurs in a job that called for experienced professionals . . .

Ten minutes later, Calvin found a parking space in a road lined with cars. They left the van, walked up the pavement to a narrow passage that took them through to the path that ran between the tiny yards of two rows of terrace houses.

Calvin came to a stop in front of a door, set in a wooden fence, that had begun to rot and had to be lifted before it could be swung inwards. 'Masks and gloves.'

There were no street lights along the passage and the yard was dark. He switched on a pencil torch which provided just enough light for them to make their way through the rubbish. He came to a halt by the back door, brought the gun from his pocket, knocked on the door. There was no response. Burrell was out, Timothy thought with a surge of relief. They'd tried, they'd failed through no fault of their own, and now they could forget the madness . . .

The window to the right of the door lit up. Burrell called out: 'Who is it?'

'Police.'

'What d'you want? I ain't . . .'

'Open up.'

A lock clicked and this was followed by the metallic noise of a chain moving along its restraining slide, then the door was opened. 'Why d'you . . .' Burrell choked on the words as he saw their masked heads.

Calvin pushed his way inside. 'One shout and I'll blow your brains out.'

Sweat broke out on Burrell's forehead and face and an eyelid began to twitch to a nervous tic. Both Calvin and Timothy were shocked to hear voices from the next room, but before shock could turn into panic they realized from the even fluency of the voices that they were listening to television.

Timothy shut the door and drew the faded, tattered curtain across the window.

'On the floor,' Calvin ordered.

Burrell was making animal noises as he collapsed, rather than sank, on the floor to the side of a table that was littered with the debris of past meals. 'I ain't got no money,' he whimpered.

'You'll write a confession admitting you raped Miss Hurst.'

'It wasn't me. On me mother's grave, it wasn't.'

Calvin produced a sheet of paper and a ballpoint pen, put them down on the floor.

'I was with me mates all night.'

'You've one minute to grow sensible.'

Burrell was sweating so heavily, he might have recently come in from the rain.

'Tie him up and gag him.'

Timothy, feeling that this was a nightmare which

robbed him of all free will, brought from his pockets a length of string, a duster and a scarf.

He jammed the duster into Burrell's mouth with considerably more force than he'd intended because the stench was sickening, tied the scarf so that it held the duster in place. 'Turn over.' He secured Burrell's wrists together with the string, then rolled him back.

Calvin put the gun in one pocket, brought the Elejumper from another. He held the small black box, three inches long, two wide, with two stubby metal rods at the far end, above Burrell's face. 'It gives an electrical shock. Applied to wet skin it makes a man feel that his muscles are being torn apart.' He pressed the button on the side and blue lightning streaked between the rods. He lowered it until it was only two inches above Burrell's nose, pressed the button again. Burrell screamed, but the gag reduced the noise to a dull wailing.

'Are you ready to write?'

He thrashed around violently and drummed on the floor with the heels of his shoes.

'Hold him or the whole bloody neighbourhood'll be along.'

Timothy grabbed Burrell and managed to subdue him.

Calvin rested the prongs on Burrell's nose. 'You're sweating so hard, I'll not need to wet your skin first.'

'You said, no . . .' began Timothy urgently.

'*Ferme ta gueule.*'

He realized he'd stupidly been about to destroy any chance they had of breaking Burrell's resistance.

Calvin said: 'Ten seconds, then I press the switch.'

Several seconds had passed when he suddenly lifted the Elejumper and swung round to look at the window. 'What was that?'

'What?' Timothy replied thickly.

'That noise . . . Turn the light off and look outside.'

He switched off the overhead light, pulled the corner of the curtain aside. As his eyes became accustomed to the dark, he could just make out that the yard was empty. 'No one.'

'Go outside and keep watch, just in case.'

He hesitated.

'Tie his legs and he can't go anywhere.'

That was not why he'd been hesitating. He switched on the light. To the right of the sink there was a rag that proved to be long enough to secure Burrell's feet.

'Bang on the door if there's an alarm.'

He switched off the light, opened the door, stepped outside and closed the door behind himself. When the light inside was switched back on, he moved to his right because the shadows were deeper there. After a while, he thought he heard sounds from inside, similar to those which Burrell had made earlier when trying to scream, but they were too indistinct for him to be certain.

Finally, the light went out, the door opened, and Calvin stepped out. 'He became very cooperative.'

There had been a note almost of exaltation in his voice, Timothy thought.

16

Metcalf parked his car in the reserved bay, crossed to the side door, entered the building and climbed the stairs to the fifth floor instead of taking the lift. Having promised his wife that he'd take more exercise, ease off on the work, and spend more time at home with the family, it was a chance to honour one of those promises.

More out of breath than he should have been, he sat behind his desk and stared at the mail, but for the moment did not touch it. Retirements and promotions to senior ranks were posted at the beginning of August and he'd been given the rumour that he was in line for detective chief inspector at county HQ. Would he get that promotion? He was not being conceited to tell himself that he deserved to; he was being realistic when he remembered the Tyrell case and accepted that this might count against him too much.

He opened the mail, sorting the letters, internal memoranda, and external pamphlets, into those which needed some immediate action on his part, could wait, needed filing, or could be consigned to the wastepaper basket. The sixth envelope was typewritten and addressed to the detective inspector. Instinctively – and he could not easily have explained this – he opened the envelope with the paper knife his daughter had given him for his last birthday and brought out the single sheet of crumpled paper by its edges. He used the paper knife once more to unfold the paper, read the scrawled confession. He used the internal phone to call Grey.

'Read that, but don't touch it.'

'What the hell? It's got to be a hoax.'

'You don't imagine he suffered a sudden conscience? Can't say I do, either.'

Naylor parked and walked along to number eleven and knocked on the door; a fleck of paint broke off and wriggled down to the ground. As he waited, he hoped Hazel, who'd been sick twice before he'd left home, really was all right. If he'd been in charge of composing the world, he'd have made pregnancy and birth a far simpler process; kangaroos had the right idea. He knocked again.

He walked along to the next house and rang the bell. Almost immediately, the door was opened by a short, dumpy woman who was wearing an apron. 'Sorry to bother you, love, but I'm wondering if you know where your neighbour is? I can't get an answer.'

'Haven't you heard? They took him off to hospital.'

'Why's that?'

'He fell downstairs and hurt himself real bad. It was me that found him and called the ambulance,' she said proudly. 'There was this knocking on the wall, see. Bill – that's the husband – said he'd give Rudy a piece of his mind for making so much noise, but I didn't want no trouble so I went round to the back to ask him to stop. The door wasn't locked, so I stuck me head into the kitchen and that's when I sees him. Fair give me a turn, with him lying on the floor, knocking on the wall with his feet. Didn't know where to look.'

'He didn't?'

'I didn't. On account of him not having any trousers on.'

He doubted she'd been even a quarter embarrassed as she wanted him to believe. 'Would you know which hospital they took him to?'

'Can't say. General, like as not.'

'Thanks for all your help.' He returned to the car, used

104

the radio to tell divisional HQ that he was off to Southwold General Hospital.

Reception directed him to L ward. As he entered the long, brightly-lit ward, he wondered why it was that ever since Hazel's pregnancy had advanced to the nail-biting stage, he'd had to spend time in hospitals? Breaking him in? He introduced himself to the nurse who sat at a desk at the near end and said he'd like a chat with Burrell.

'I suppose it's all right,' she said doubtfully.

'What state's he in?'

'A lot of pain. And telling everyone just how much,' she added, with professional disapproval for someone who did not suffer his agony stoically.

'What exactly are his injuries?'

'A fractured cheekbone, two cracked ribs, heavy bruising, and a badly swollen testicle.'

'Then it's small wonder he's moaning! How could he damage that vital piece of machinery when falling downstairs?'

'You'll have to ask him, not me.'

'Which bed is he in?'

'The fourth on the left.' Then, in a friendly gesture, she added: 'If I were you, I'd make certain to keep your distance.'

'Because of his breath? Don't worry, I'll stay well to windward.'

She did not miss the significance of the fact that clearly he had known Burrell previously.

He walked down the ward to the fourth bed, did not sit on the chair since this would have meant he would have been on a level with Burrell's mouth.

'What d'you want?' Burrell demanded with sharp, defensive fear.

'I'm here to sympathize. How come you fell downstairs?'

'Tripped.'

'And turned head over heels, catching your nuts on the bannisters?'

Silence.

'Is there anything you'd like to tell me?'

'Yeah. Piss off.'

'Sorry you feel like that. But don't give up hope. Eventually, the swelling may die down so you're no longer lopsided.'

Naylor walked back to the nurse at the desk. 'Would you know what doctor treated him?'

'Dr Sayles.'

'Is it possible to have a word with him?'

She looked at her fob watch. 'He'll be off duty very soon, but you could ask the receptionist to bleep him . . . Is something up?'

'Not really. I'm just curious.'

'I can see that,' she snapped, noticing that his gaze was fixed on the V of her frock.

He returned to the ground floor and spoke to the duty receptionist. Some fifteen minutes later, a tall, very swarthy man, dressed in sports clothes, went up to the desk, then crossed to where Naylor sat. 'I'm Dr Sayles.'

Naylor stood.

'Could you make it as brief as possible? I'm on my way out.'

'I'll make it just one question, Doc. Were Burrell's injuries caused by falling downstairs?'

Sayles ran the fingers of his right hand through his long, black hair. 'Presumably, you have a specific reason for asking? I'd like to know what that is before answering.'

'I'm wondering if he did not fall, but was beaten up?'

'If that's what happened, wouldn't he say so?'

'In the circumstances, maybe not.'

'I see.' He thought for a moment. 'I can't claim to be any sort of an expert when it comes to identifying the causes of injuries, but I was surprised that falling downstairs should inflict those he's suffered. Which is not to say that I was sufficiently surprised definitely to doubt him. Some of the injuries we are faced with are impossible until we meet them.'

'Would an expert be able to identify their cause?'

'Find your expert and ask him.'

'Good thinking,' said Metcalf.

He'd like that in writing, Naylor thought, remembering some of the past criticism he'd received at the DI's hands.

'We'll arrange an examination by someone experienced in the field.' Metcalf drummed his fingers on the desk. The Hurst case was beginning to look as if it might come back from the cold.

The forensic pathologist was driven by police car to Burrell's house. A cautious, pedantic man, he sorely tried the patience of the PC as he carefully examined, and then re-examined, the staircase and its surround. Eventually, however, he decided he'd seen enough and asked to be taken to the hospital.

Sayles introduced him to Burrell as a noted specialist in trauma who wished to make an examination in order that everyone could be certain that the patient was obtaining the best possible treatment.

Delighted to be the recipient of such concern, Burrell answered every question without much thought.

Metcalf, receiver to his left ear, said: 'You've no doubts?'

'None with regard to the fractured cheekbone, cracked ribs, and heavy bruising,' replied the pathologist. 'All are inconsistent with his having fallen down the stairs in his house; all are consistent with his having been assaulted. One bruise in particular, to his side, still shows qualities associated with a heavy kick from the toe of a shoe. The injury to the testicle, however, suggests a very different cause.

'Some time ago, Inspector, I was concerned with a case in which a man had had electricity applied to parts of his body and in particular to his testicles. The resultant injuries were consistent with those Burrell has suffered to his right testicle.'

'In addition to being brutally kicked, Burrell was tortured?'

'That is a probability.'

'Have you any idea what sort of equipment would have been used?'

'I can offer no certainty, only the possibility that it was one of those small machines carried in self-defence. They work off an ordinary battery, yet can deliver an extremely sharp and painful shock; a shock which, of course, becomes far worse if the skin is wet.'

Metcalf thanked the other, rang off. They now had an explanation for Burrell's otherwise inexplicable confession. One or more men, determined to make Burrell admit he was the rapist, had cornered him in the house, demanded he write a confession, tried to break his defiance by kicking him, had finally used torture until the agony had become so great that he had had to do what they demanded.

The torturers had forced the confession out of Burrell in order that he could finally be arrested, charged, and found guilty of raping Penelope Hurst. It was bitterly ironic that by obtaining the confession through torture, they had ensured that it could never be used in court.

He left his room and went next door to the detective sergeant's. Grey was struggling with the duty rosters, trying to balance shifts when men were away sick, on leave, or on courses. Metcalf sat on the edge of the desk. 'The pathologist's report adds up to the fact that Burrell was tortured into making his confession when straightforward assault by kicking failed.'

Grey whistled. 'That puts a dozen cats amongst the pigeons!'

'Quite. Send the confession letter to Dabs. Do we have Burrell's prints?'

'No.'

'Then get them, preferably without his knowing.'

17

Hospitals did not cause Tyler any uneasiness; it was not in his character to allow them to remind him of his mortality. Even the sight of the man in the bed next to Burrell, who surely had his hand outstretched to greet the angel of death, did not make him mentally wince. He was about to settle on the chair between the beds when he remembered Naylor's warning. 'I've come to ask you to do something for us.'

Burrell automatically began to deny anything and everything.

'No call to tie your knickers into a granny knot. All I'm asking is if you can recognize this writing?' He brought an envelope from his pocket, extracted a sheet of paper on which Grey had written a couple of sentences in pencil, held this out.

Burrell took the paper, looked at it briefly, handed it back. 'Ain't never seen it before.'

Careful to hold the paper by its edges, Tyler returned it to the envelope. 'Thanks.'

'That's all?' Burrell was worried. His rat-like instincts suggested that somehow he'd been made to look a right charlie.

Despite the general belief to the contrary, Dabs could – when pressed by a senior officer – work quickly. They used the latest laser scanning equipment to search for prints on the confession and on the piece of paper which Tyler had passed to Burrell in hospital. Comparison showed that two of the prints on the confession – one good, one not so good – were Burrell's.

Susan Mortimer hurried from the main hospital block across to the red Cavalier. As she pulled open the front passenger door and sat, she said: 'Sorry, Mike.'

'No sweat,' Mike replied. 'There's nothing I like better than sitting here and watching the world go round.'

'There's no call to bitch. I'm only ten minutes late.'

'Twenty-three.'

'I just couldn't get away on time.'

He started the engine. 'I suppose the great panjandrum needed you to assuage his needs?'

'Don't start that again.'

'Doctors think nurses are part of their perks.'

'You've been watching too many TV sit-coms.' She leaned across to kiss his cheek. 'Forgive?'

'So there's cause for me to forgive?'

'Only me being late. Life's been far too busy for anything else.'

He backed out of the bay, drove across the car park. 'I thought we might have a meal at Luigi's,' he said, signalling a truce.

'Lead on, Macduff.'

'Lay on.'

'Whichever. I'll sell my soul any day of the week for their chocolate ice-cream sundae.'

'So what price your body?'

She giggled. Then she said, as he braked to a halt at the gates: 'Gawd, it really has been a day! Half the population breaking bones, burning themselves, suffering cardiac arrests, or blowing up a testicle.'

'Doing what?'

'A man came in with one the size of an egg.'

'It hurts just to hear about it. How the hell did he manage that?'

'He says he fell downstairs.'

'I'll move into a bungalow.'

'But the talk is, he was tortured.'

'Tell me more,' he said, as he drove out on to the road.

'His breath stinks.'

'Never mind that.'

'You'd mind one hell of a lot if you had to suffer it . . . He came in semi-conscious and with heavy bruising, a fractured cheekbone, a couple of damaged ribs, and the swollen testicle. None of us thought that much about it until a detective questioned him and another doctor was called in to examine him and the buzz went round that he was heard telling Dr Sayles that there was no doubt almost all the injuries were due to kicking, but that the swollen testicle had probably been caused by the application of electricity.'

'What d'you know about this bloke?'

'Nothing.'

'You've no idea why he might have been tortured?'

'Of course not.'

'I thought patients told you everything when you cradled them to your soft, creamy bosom.'

'You're a male chauvinistic optimist.'

'How did you guess? It sounds to be worth following up.'

Metcalf sat behind his desk; Grey and Naylor stood in front of it. Metcalf said: 'Burrell was identified as the rapist by someone who was in a position to judge that he could not be arrested whilst his alibi stood; and that someone was so determined he should be brought to justice that he tortured Burrell into writing the confession . . . What's our next move?'

'We use the confession to pressure him into giving us one that will stand up in court,' Grey said.

'It could be worth the try. No further comment?'

'I suppose that if it's proved he was tortured . . .'

'Once he understands the situation, he will rush to admit that he was in order to make his existing confession inadmissible. So we're going to have to identify his torturer.'

'Why?' asked Naylor.

'Is that a serious question?'

'Yes, sir.'

'You really need to have the reason explained?'

Naylor knew he'd be a fool to say anything more; nevertheless, he said it. 'He raped Miss Hurst and put her through hell. If he's been handed a touch of hell, that's fair enough.'

'I'll forget that.' In his mind, Metcalf agreed with Naylor; outwardly though, he had to condemn such a position. A policeman's life contained even more hypocrisy than the average man's. 'Burrell must be questioned. Once we have his evidence, we'll try to identify his torturer. It should not prove difficult since that person must have had the motive and been in a position to understand that Burrell would have been arrested had he not had an alibi. Can either of you suggest a possible suspect other than Calvin Slade?'

Grey said: 'No, sir.' Naylor, his expression sullen, shook his head.

'Very well. But remember, Calvin's father is a very powerful, very influential man. So no short cuts.'

They questioned Burrell less than two hours after he had been discharged from hospital. They did not carry hypocrisy so far as to express any sorrow at seeing him still in considerable pain. They remained standing, he sat slumped on a chair whose cover was threadbare and stained with grease.

'We know you didn't fall downstairs,' Grey said.

'I did,' Burrell muttered.

'Then if you weren't tortured, why d'you write out a confession?'

Burrell's expression of dismay was almost laughable. 'I ain't confessed to anything.'

'Seems like with all the aches and pains, you'd forgotten

about it.' Grey turned to Naylor. 'Show him the copy to jog his memory.'

Naylor handed a photocopy to Burrell.

'I don't know nothing about this. Never seen it. It's a bleeding fake.'

'Then I wonder why your dabs are on the original?'

Burrell began to sweat.

'Maybe no one's ever explained the laws of evidence to you? Your confession is admissible if made voluntarily and because you were seized by the desire to pay your debt to society. It is inadmissible if made from the threat, or the actual application, of force.'

He hurriedly told them what had happened.

Three-quarters of an hour later, Naylor at the wheel, they drove away from number eleven.

'If I had my way . . .' began Naylor.

'Look, Fred, the Old Man could have roasted you this morning for what you said; don't risk any more.'

'You don't reckon . . .'

'I've enough common that what I reckon, I keep to myself.' He brought out his pipe, put it in his mouth, but did not light it. 'It was always odds on that it was the two of 'em. Stupid sods.'

'You can't understand what made 'em do it?'

'I can understand, I can sympathize, and I can still call 'em stupid sods. They've gained nothing when it comes to arresting Burrell and they're for the high jump.'

'It could be difficult to turn up sufficient evidence to prove it was them.'

'A strong word of advice. Play things straight or it'll be you who hits the fan.'

'Maybe my middle name's Nelson.'

'He won that battle; you'll lose this one. Makes all the difference.' He produced a box of matches and struck one.

Naylor lowered his window to its fullest extent.

*　　　*　　　*

113

As Timothy entered the house, there was a call from the kitchen. He went through. 'Calvin rang,' Christine said. 'He wants you to get back on to him right away.'

'Thanks.'

'Is something wrong?'

'No. Why d'you keep asking?'

'Because I'm worried.'

'There's no reason to be.'

She used a wooden spoon to stir the contents of a plastic bowl. 'You are quite sure of that?'

'Would you like a sworn statement?'

'It's just that . . . Calvin's rung you twice before and from the way he spoke this time, you've not got back to him.'

'I haven't.'

'For any particular reason?'

'Just that I want to concentrate on work.' She was wondering whether something had happened to strain the friendship. And almost certainly hoping that it had.

'What's cooking?' he asked, to change the subject.

'Nick's missed out on lunch so I'm making a steam pudding.'

'How's the new work?'

'He thinks there's a good chance that it'll lead to bigger and better things.'

'That would be really great.'

'Wouldn't it? It would do his ego so much good. Sometimes, he gets really downhearted . . .' She stopped.

'Why won't you let me put the degree on hold and find a job?'

'Without that all-important piece of paper, what sort of job would you get with the market as difficult as it is at the moment? If you ended up clerking, we'd both feel that everything would have been . . . wasted.'

She played that card every time, knowing how loath he would be to cause her and his father such distress; when she wanted something for someone else, she was prepared

114

to go to any lengths to gain it; if for herself, she would scorn any form of subterfuge.

He left the kitchen and made his way up to his bedroom where he sat at the small desk, picked up an opened text book and began to read. After a moment, he put the book down, aware that he had not taken in a single word. Did Calvin keep phoning because the memories were as painful for him? He must have been equally sickened by the sight of Burrell reduced by terror to a moaning wreck. Both of them had learned something. Revenge truly was a kind of wild justice that needed weeding out.

18

As time passed, the detectives and PCs on the house-to-house were overtaken by boredom and their minds wandered even as they asked for the umpteenth time, had the person to whom they were speaking seen on the night of Friday before last an old, open four-seater car, green, with aeroscreens, an outside handbrake, a strap over the bonnet, and a large silver radiator?

'Ain't never seen anything like that round here,' said the middle-aged woman, a little too large for the clothes she wore, her features hard, her manner belligerent. 'But there was this van parked in front of the house . . .'

'Thanks very much,' said PC Young.

She was not silenced that easily. 'What I want to know is, what was it doing right where Bert always leaves our car? Why don't you lot stop it?'

'We can't prevent parking where people can find a space, not in a road where there aren't any restrictions . . .'

'It's always the same. When we want something done, you lot tells us you can't do it. Bert always parks in front, like everyone does. So when we come back after being with our Fran because her husband's a good-for-nothing and her with a new kid and two already to cope with . . .'

'I really can't help.'

'Because the likes of us don't matter.'

Young wondered why he always seemed to get them? 'You matter just as much as anyone else.'

'Then why d'you let the van park in our place?'

'I suppose the driver returned home and couldn't find room in front of his own house.'

'There ain't no one here who works for that firm.'

'Then he was visiting.'

'Visiting in a van like that? It shouldn't be allowed, so why don't you stop it?'

'So long as it wasn't illegal because of its size . . .'

'Bert had to park right down at the bottom of the road.'

'In front of someone else's house?'

'D'you think there's a multi-storey car park there?'

'That's what happens . . .'

'I'll tell you what happens. A van sits in front of us so we can't park. If Bert could've got downstairs quick enough, he'd have said a thing or two to the driver, only he was in bed and it took time after we heard the van doors. Drove off just as he opened the front door. Proper mad that made him.'

'Then probably it's just as well it did leave smartly.'

'And the driver couldn't drive. Why d'you let people park where they shouldn't when they don't even know how to drive?'

Young suddenly realized that perhaps her belligerent complaints might be significant. 'What makes you so sure the driver didn't know how to drive it?'

'Bert said he steered all over the road and couldn't change gear. You want to call Bert a liar?'

'The last thing I'd dream of doing.' Van drivers often 'borrowed' their vans, even large ones, to return home or visit friends, but then, by definition, they would not drive like tyros. 'What sort of time did all this happen?'

'We left Fran just about midnight.'

'How long did it take you to drive back here?'

'Ten minutes.'

'Did you look at the van?'

'Had to, to know it was there, didn't I?' she said scornfully.

'What I meant was, did you notice any name on its side?'

'I told you, Jenton Coldstores.'

She'd not mentioned that before, but he wasn't going to correct her. 'Thanks. You've been a great help.'

'Then suppose you make certain it don't park there again.'

Grey listened to Young's report. 'It could've been someone visiting,' he observed.

'When the driver made such a BU on leaving?'

'Never crashed the gears of your car?'

The PC was unwilling to accept that perhaps he had not uncovered a very significant piece of evidence. 'The time's right and Peartree Crescent is the next road.'

'I'm not forgetting that . . . Tell you what. Nip across town and have a word with someone at the coldstore and find out if they know if one of their vans was out that night.'

The manager of the Southwold branch of Jenton Coldstores shook his head. 'The company rules say no private use of vans.'

'So where are they kept at night?' Young asked.

'At the back, under cover.'

One of the two phones on the desk rang and the manager picked it up, listened, spoke with brief anger, replaced the receiver. 'If there are two ways of doing it, they choose the wrong one.'

From the look of him, Young thought, he had a mean, sharp nature. 'Could someone have taken a van out that night without your knowing?'

'A few years back we used smaller ones and the drivers were always sneaking off with 'em at night; now, they have to clock out and in and the ignition keys are kept in my office.'

'One of your vans was parked in Keir Street around midnight.'

'No way.'

'It had your name on the side.'

'Then it was from one of the other depots.'

'Or someone broke in here and borrowed it.'

'If there'd been any signs of a break-in, I'd have been on to you blokes to report it.'

Young had a dogged character. 'Who's in charge of making certain the vans are returned at night and the keys handed in?'

'Jim Arundell.'

'Could I have a word with him?'

'If you must.'

Arundell was a dried-up man in late middle age. Young spoke to him in the yard to the side of the end building. 'Was any of the vans out on the night of Friday before last?'

'No.' He removed the gloves he had been wearing and unzipped the insulated jacket because the sunshine was warm. 'I do me job right.'

'D'you work every Saturday?'

'Got to.'

'So did you notice anything different about any of the vans on the Saturday morning?'

'How d'you mean?'

'Were there any signs of fresh damage or did any of 'em give trouble?'

'No.'

'So nothing had changed?'

He scratched the top of his head, at the apex of the V of baldness. 'There was only the key.'

'What key was that?'

'I hang 'em all in the manager's office before I leave for home, like he wants. Always put 'em on the same hooks. One of 'em had been moved.'

'Are you certain?'

''Course I am.'

'You couldn't have been interrupted by something on the Friday evening as you were hanging up that key and you put it on a different hook because you were in a hurry?'

'No.'

Grey watched Young leave and thought that he'd looked disappointed, as if he'd expected an illuminated address extolling his sharp initiative. Nevertheless, for someone in uniform it had been a smart piece of work . . .

The vans were kept in a lean-to in a yard formed by brick walls, one of the sheds, and heavy chain-link fencing; the two gates were secured by padlock. On the Saturday morning, the padlock had been fast, the chain in place, and the fencing undamaged. Young's judgement was that the padlock was of sufficiently robust design to call for a competent screwsman to force it. So how could a rank amateur open it and then relock it unless he had a key?

Grey dialled, spoke to the retired sergeant who was in charge of Information at County HQ – a department introduced by the chief constable four years before to derisory comment – and asked for information on Jenton Coldstores. Three-quarters of an hour later, he was told that Jenton Coldstores were part of Bretton & Freeland; the chairman of this conglomerate was Steven Slade . . .

'Well, well!' he said to the wall as he replaced the receiver. He thought for a while, then looked in the local directory for Jenton Coldstores' Southwold number. He told the sharp-voiced secretary that he'd like to speak to the manager.

'What is it this time?' demanded the manager.

'Has Mr Calvin Slade ever worked at your place?'

'Why are you asking?'

'Just routine.'

There was a long pause, then the manager said: 'He recently spent a few weeks here.'

'Working?'

'Am I to be quoted?'

'No.'

Word had come down from on high, said the manager,

120

that Mr Calvin Slade was joining the holding company and so that he might learn about the day-to-day running of the various subsidiaries, he would be spending some time working with each. He had been at the Southwold branch for six weeks. In that time, it was doubtful that he had bothered to learn anything.

'But he would have discovered where the keys of the vans were kept?'

'He had every opportunity to do so. Whether he treated that opportunity with the same contempt as all the others, I've no idea.'

Grey thanked the other, rang off. He wrote a brief note and left this on the DI's desk.

Metcalf ordered another house-to-house, this time to determine whether anyone had seen the van's arrival or departure. To prove the truth of the old adage that the suburbs never slept, it turned out that a couple had followed the van into Keir Street.

'When I saw it stopping, I said to Will, Bert and Trudy's car's not there so they ain't at home; they won't like it parking in front of their house.' She turned to her husband. 'I said that, didn't I?'

'That you did,' he replied briefly.

'I thought maybe we ought to tell 'em. I mean, Bert's quick to speak and he can be real mean. But Will said, best let be. That's what you said, ain't it, Will?'

He nodded.

Naylor began to understand why his expression was somewhat morose. 'Did you see who was driving the van?'

'Not at first, because like I said, we was behind. But when we was past and Will had parked, I looked back and there was these two men walking on the pavement.'

'Can you be sure they came from the van?'

'They must have done. I mean, there wasn't anyone else around. There wasn't was there, Will?'

'No.'

'Can you describe them – height, build, what they were wearing?'

'They was quite a way away.'

'Try your best.'

Her face screwed up as she thought back. 'They was both taller than Will. And bigger. You know, broader. Wouldn't you say they was bigger, Will?'

'Aye.'

'Were they about the same height?'

'I'd say they was. I mean, there wasn't much difference. Or would you say one was just that little bit taller than the other, Will?'

'Could be.'

'What about the colour and style of their hair?'

'They was too far away to tell. You see, the street lighting ain't all that good, not since lads smashed two of 'em and the council's not been along to repair 'em. There's been no one along, has there, Will?'

Her husband made no response.

'What kind of clothes were they wearing?'

She rubbed the large mole on her cheek, then fiddled with the single hair which grew out of it. 'They looked the same. Dark. A sort of overalls . . . Wouldn't you say they was like overalls only smarter, Will?'

'Didn't look.'

'And as far as you can say, they walked to the end of the road?'

'Not then. They turned into the alley what leads to the track which runs between the houses in this road and the ones in Peartree Crescent.'

Inquiries were carried out in the vicinity of the coldstore. Once again, luck ran with the police.

'I've seen a W.O. Bentley in front of the office,' said the red-headed man, as he stood in the doorway of his house. 'It wasn't all that long ago.'

'How can you be sure it was a Bentley?' asked the PC.

'No mistaking it; a four and a half. Wasn't a three, a six or an eight.'

The PC had no idea what that meant. 'Can you place the day and time?'

'Look, come on in instead of standing there. Jenny can likely help; women are better at this sort of thing.'

The PC followed him into a room filled with new white pine furniture and bright colour. They were joined by a young woman, smartly dressed, whose possessive glances at her husband suggested a recent marriage. When the question was put to her, she answered without hesitation. 'It was a week ago last Friday. You were back late and then kept me up half the night telling me about the old crock you'd seen on the way home.'

'Vintage heirloom.'

'Give me a Volvo any day.'

'That shows a complete and utter lack of taste.'

'It shows a complete and utter liking for something that works and is comfortable.'

The PC hastened to break up an argument that clearly was time-honoured. 'What sort of time would this have been?'

She answered. 'It must have been a little after eleven. I'd waited downstairs until the end of the programme on the telly, then went on up. My husband came in very soon after that.'

The PC turned to the husband. 'And how long before you arrived home would you have seen the Bentley?'

'Must have been around ten minutes. At that time of night, the traffic's light.'

The PC had no idea whether the information was of great, little, or no importance.

19

Christine called up from the hall: 'Tim, it's Calvin.'

Timothy inserted a marker, closed the book. If Mahomet wouldn't go to the mountain . . . He stood, crossed to the door and stepped out on to the landing as Calvin reached the head of the stairs.

'So you're still alive,' Calvin said aggressively.

'As far as I can tell. But could I know I wasn't if I were not?'

'I've phoned a dozen times.'

'Christine mentioned you'd rung thrice.'

'So why the hell didn't you get back on to me?'

'I've been above my eyebrows in work.' He stepped back into the bedroom.

Calvin followed him, shut the door. 'Have you heard anything?'

'Not a whisper.'

'Why isn't his arrest in the papers?'

'Isn't it? We only have *The Times*. That prefers articles on Thomas Eakin to rape.'

'Who the hell's he?'

'An American painter.'

'What's he to do with Burrell?'

'Nothing.'

'You've a bloody lousy sense of humour.' Calvin slumped down on the corner of the bed.

Timothy sat on the chair in front of the desk. 'Have you heard from Penny?'

'No.'

'I had a card this morning. The weather's marvellous and the food's so good she'll put on a stone if she can't develop some self-control. She's obviously a lot more cheerful. That's great, isn't it?'

'Maybe the confession's been lost in the post.'

'Far more likely that the police are working things out before they give the news of the confession to the public.'

'Work what out? Arrest the bastard and sling him into jail.'

'They have to be certain there's sufficient evidence to satisfy the Crown Prosecution Service . . . Will you tell me something?'

'What?'

'What went through your mind when Burrell was lying on the floor of the kitchen, absolutely petrified?'

Calvin stared at him. 'What d'you think was going through it?'

'I don't know. That's why I'm asking.'

'I was working out how best to make him confess.'

'Then you didn't . . . didn't wonder how you could be doing what you were? How you could have deliberately terrified another human being?'

'Are you trying to take the mickey out of me?'

'It's a serious question.'

'Then you need a psychiatrist.'

'That could be right.'

Calvin stood. 'You've got softening of the brain from too much work. Relax and come for a spin?'

'I'd like to, but I can't. Unlike you, my future is only assured if I get a really good degree and then find a rich man's daughter who wants to marry me.'

'Get her in pod and she'll cooperate . . . Not had any word from the police, I suppose?'

'Not yet.'

'Even if that bastard screams his head off, they're all so thick they won't get anywhere.'

'I hope you're right.'

125

'You remember what to say if they start asking questions?'

'Isn't that irrelevant since you've just assured me they won't?'

'Jesus, you can be goddamn stupid! . . . You turned up at home around seven. Fenella was there, Dad wasn't because he was in France trying to get a bunch of Frogs to do business. We had dinner and then played Trivial Pursuit. I won two games and you won one.'

'Aren't you going to allow Fenella any glory?'

'I wish I could make you out,' Calvin said angrily. 'Instead of being so smart-arsed, suppose you remember that after playing, we watched a tape – *Seven Brides For Seven Brothers . . .*'

'You don't think that the Kamasutra On Ice would sound more plausible?'

Calvin left the room, slamming the door behind himself. After a moment, Timothy heard the roar of the Bentley being revved in neutral, then the diminishing boom of its four-inch diameter exhaust as it drove off. He wondered why he'd been so naïve as to ask Calvin what his thoughts had been when he'd stared down at the terrified Burrell?

Mortimer was a reporter on the *Southwold Courier*, a local newspaper with a surprisingly healthy circulation that was part of a county combine. For him, life was for enjoying, not just living; but he was ambitious and ready to work hard. Ever since Susan had told him about the possibility of Burrell's having been tortured, he'd been trying to find out what, when and why. A phone call on Monday morning from one of his contacts at divisional police HQ began to answer the questions.

'Burrell definitely was tortured. According to him, that was to force him to make a confession.'

'A confession to what?'

'The rape of Penelope Hurst.'

126

Mortimer whistled.

'Two masked men broke into his house and used him as a football and jammed an electrical probe on his testicle with the power turned high.'

'That's really hitting below the belt! Are there any leads on who the two men were?'

'No one's saying, but you don't need to be a genius to work out that one of 'em was Penelope Hurst's boyfriend, Calvin Slade.'

'The money Slade?'

'Only son of.'

'This is becoming more exciting than sex. Has son Calvin been questioned?'

'Not yet.'

'Playing it very carefully?'

'Wouldn't you?'

'Until I was dead certain . . . George, it looks like you've come up with all trumps.'

After replacing the receiver, Mortimer stared into space. Another vigilante case? And one which would grab the great British reading public by their prurient souls? If so, this story was going to make the nationals.

Metcalf walked into Grey's room. 'We need to trace the purchase of the ski-masks.'

Grey put the ballpoint pen down by the side of an open folder. 'Do you want me to organize inquiries at all possible outlets?'

'That may not be necessary.' Metcalf walked over to the window and stared out. 'You've met Calvin Slade. What's your picture of him?'

'Arrogant, spoiled rotten.'

'There's no call to flatter.' He turned round. 'Where do really superior people do their shopping? In those emporia where the staff are trained to appreciate their superiority. Where do you find such shops? Not in Southwold, which has dissented ever since the time of Jack Cade; in London. Which is the most chic store in London for winter sports?

127

Straw and Nielson . . . I'll offer you odds on that when Calvin Stone decided he needed a couple of ski-masks, it never occurred to him to buy them anywhere but there. Find out if I win the bet.'

Straw and Nielson's window display consisted of an oil painting depicting Mount Everest with a trailing plume of snow – they did not seek casual trade. Inside, the accent was on designer clothes as much as, or perhaps more than, equipment.

'May I help you . . . sir?' said the assistant, leaving a sufficient gap between the last two words to make the 'sir' a reluctant afterthought.

'CID,' replied Blake curtly, being a labour-voting democrat. 'I want a word with the boss.'

'I will ascertain if Miss Aitchson is free.'

The manageress was younger and very much more attractive than Blake – also a male chauvinist – had expected. 'Would you like to come through to my office?'

The room was functionally furnished and the only touch of femininity was a cut glass vase of flowers. She sat behind the kidney-shaped desk. 'How exactly can I help you?'

'We've been asked to find out if you've recently sold two ski-masks to a certain person. We're hoping you'll remember if you have because it's an unusual time of the year for anyone to buy them.'

'Not really, you know. Skiing in the southern hemisphere is very popular and we regularly increase our summer sales.'

How the other one per cent lived!

'But I'll do what I can to help. What is the name?'

'Calvin Slade.'

'I'll check the records.' She swivelled her chair round to face a desk-top computer, switched that on, tapped several keys. She studied the screen, pressed another key and the display rolled. 'Mr Slade bought two ski-masks and two ski-suits on Thursday, the eighth.'

'You can be quite certain of that?'

'He paid by credit card.'

It was, Blake thought, astonishing how stupid the rich could be.

20

The front doorbell rang. Timothy heard, but took no notice of it. The case law concerning the construction of documents demanded all his concentration; at times, when the arcane subtleties became very great, perhaps more than he possessed.

'Tim,' his mother called out.

'What's up?' He tried not to sound as irritated as he felt; just for a moment – before her call – he'd thought he'd grasped the difference between 'will be' as used in document A and 'will be' as used in document B.

'There's someone wants to talk to you.'

Had the caller been Calvin, she would have said so – if there had been time to do so before Calvin arrogantly assumed the invitation to go straight up; none of his other friends would interrupt work. There had been a strange note in her voice, as if the caller were both unexpected and unwelcome . . .

Christine was waiting in the hall. 'They are two local detectives.'

He was momentarily shocked and panicky.

'What's the matter?'

He pulled himself together. 'Nothing.'

'What do they want?'

'I suppose it's more questions concerning Penny.' He made a joke of the fear he had had only a moment before. 'I doubt they're here to arrest me.'

Relieved, she smiled. 'I certainly hope they aren't. Not when I'm cooking Cumberland hotpot.'

'If that's on the menu, I'll get rid of them in double-quick time.' He opened the door of the sitting room and went in. He recognized both men, without remembering their names.

As if in answer to the unasked question, Grey introduced himself and Naylor. 'Just a few questions we'd like answered.' He sounded friendly.

'If it's in connection with Penny, I expect you know she's in Florida.'

'Yes, we did. Have you heard how she is?'

'Much better.'

'That's good news. But as a matter of fact, we're here over a different matter. You'll remember who Edward Burrell is?'

'Of course.' Tension closed in on Timothy.

'A week ago last Friday, two men broke into his home. They tortured and assaulted him . . .'

'They what?' he exclaimed, before he could check himself.

'That surprises you?'

'I . . . I didn't think that sort of thing happened these days.'

'Sadly, more and more frequently. He was tortured by the application of electricity to his dampened testicle. Then he was violently kicked in the face and side.'

'But that's . . .'

'Yes?'

'No one could behave like that.'

'Naturally, we've considered the possibility that he's lying. However, the medical evidence confirms his story.'

Timothy remembered. He'd been sickened by the sight of Burrell's terror and had been about to remonstrate with Calvin when Calvin had heard a noise outside and had directed him to keep watch there. He'd heard nothing. But, only too thankful to have good reason to leave the kitchen . . . Calvin had wanted him out of the way because he had decided not to restrict himself to the threat of torture . . .

131

'Are you all right?'

He realized he had to control his racing thoughts. 'Why do you ask?'

'You looked rather bewildered.'

'It's just that I'm shocked to know people can still behave like savages.'

'I imagine I don't have to explain why Burrell was tortured?'

'You will if you want me to understand.'

'Very well. As you know, Burrell became the prime – in fact, the only – suspect in the rape of Miss Hurst. But when we questioned him, he was able to produce an alibi which eliminated him from the case. Naturally, we checked the alibi very, very thoroughly, but in the end were forced to accept it.

'This left us in a situation that's extremely frustrating, to describe it politely, but one we have to learn to live with. We're certain we know who's guilty of a crime, but because there's insufficient proof for a court of law, we cannot make the arrest. Unfortunately, the public doesn't always understand the need to be able to prove guilt beyond all reasonable doubt and certain members see the police's failure to act as a fatal weakness and they decide to correct this weakness with direct action. We call such people, vigilantes.

'However well-intentioned their motives, no matter how appalling the original crime, the hard fact is that what the vigilante does is totally illegal. So although the torture of Burrell was to force him to confess to an appalling rape, the two vigilantes were guilty of a brutal assault on him. Therefore, we have to identify them.'

'And,' said Naylor, speaking for the first time, 'we thought maybe you could help us do this.'

'Why me?' Timothy was conscious that his voice had become croaky.

'It's like this,' said Grey. 'The two vigilantes must not only have had motive, but also have been in a position to know the course of our investigation. Both you and Mr

Calvin Slade are very friendly with Miss Hurst and therefore you will have suffered emotionally when she was raped; you were aware, from your own observations and from what she was in a position to tell you, that we were unable to make an arrest only because Burrell had an alibi we could not prove was false.'

'Are . . .' He swallowed heavily. 'Are you accusing me?'

'Just asking if you can help us in our inquiries. Perhaps name someone else who was very close to Miss Hurst and who may well have known how the investigations were proceeding. Can you do that?'

'No.'

Grey brought his pipe out and began to rub the bowl against his cheek. Naylor said: 'It might be an idea if you tell us where you were that night?'

Timothy tried to give the impression of someone who wanted to help and was thinking back. 'I'm pretty certain I was at Calvin's . . . Yes, I'm sure that that's the night I was.'

'When did you get there?'

'I suppose it was somewhere around seven.'

'When did you leave?'

'I don't know exactly. Probably some time after midnight.'

'And there were just the two of you at home?'

'No. Mrs Slade was there. Mr Slade was in France.'

'She was with you throughout the evening?'

'That's right.'

The two detectives looked at each other. Grey lowered his pipe. 'Thanks for your help.' He stood. 'We'll be on our way.'

'I'll see you out.'

As Timothy closed the front door behind them, he frantically tried to assess how far they'd believed him . . . His worried thoughts were interrupted when Christine entered the hall from the kitchen and said: 'What did they want?'

'Apparently two vigilantes beat up Burrell to make him

admit he raped Penny. They wondered if they were Calvin and me.'

'Oh, my God!'

'There's no call for panic. As I told 'em, I was with Calvin and Fenella all evening.'

She ran her fingers through her hair. 'Thank God for that! Just for one second, I thought you'd been stupid enough to let Calvin lead you into real trouble.'

'No way.'

'I'm sorry, Tim. But . . .' She did not finish.

He had to talk to Calvin to ask him how he could have been so brutally, bloodily stupid, thereby making a nonsense of their whole plan. But if he phoned now, Christine would realize that events were far more serious than he'd made out.

Naylor braked to match the movements of the car ahead. Then, as he accelerated, he said: 'It's interesting how the thrust of this case is matching that in the rape one.'

'And if you reckon that's coincidence, you'd better go back on the beat,' muttered Grey.

'If Mrs Slade backs up his story, there's another alibi we're not going to break.'

'That's right.'

'That won't give me any sleepless nights.'

'When the hell are you going to learn that discretion is the better part of survival?'

Metcalf took over the questioning from Tyler. He hoped he'd be able to make Calvin contradict himself, not just for the sake of justice, but to prove that he wasn't as smart as he thought. 'You are very friendly with Miss Hurst?'

'I've already said so.'

'And she frequently talked to you about the course of the investigation?'

'I've also answered that question.'

'Then you would agree that you had a motive?'

'I've a motive for a hundred and one things which I'll never get around to doing.'

'You knew we couldn't break Burrell's alibi.'

'Couldn't be bothered to.'

'My officers spent many hours investigating the facts.'

'Then it's a pity they're so inefficient.'

'Would you like to tell us where you were that Friday night?'

'Frankly, no.'

'It might very well be in your interests.'

'I doubt it.'

'Mr Slade, it would seem that you don't appreciate the situation.'

'Situations bore me, unless they're interestingly embarrassing.'

'In the circumstances, we have to consider the possibility that you know more about the assault on Burrell than you are prepared to admit.'

'Be my guest and consider.'

'Your attitude is hardly helpful.'

'I'm not trying to help.'

'Then you must be prepared to face the consequences.'

'A threat?'

'A fact.'

'An interesting substitution.'

'Where were you throughout that Friday night?'

'Another question I've already answered.'

'On the contrary. You merely expressed a dislike of doing so. Presumably, because you find it a very difficult question to answer.'

'On the contrary,' Calvin said mockingly.

'Then what is the answer?'

'Which Friday has you so concerned?'

'The one before last.'

'Well, I'm fairly certain I wasn't in Monte Carlo. I never am. It lost all ton when the lager brigade started going there on package holidays. *Sic transit gloria mundi*, as my old assistant headmaster would say.'

'I'm interested in where you were, not where you weren't,' snapped Metcalf, aware that he was consigned to the lager brigade.

'Well, since I also wasn't in Bora Bora, I suppose I must have been here, at home.'

'On your own?'

'No.'

'With whom?'

'Never ask a gentleman that.'

'Presumably, Timothy Rees?'

'To presume is to become presumptuous. However, by chance, you're right.'

'How long was he here?'

'All evening.'

'And you've no independent witness to confirm that?'

'How independent would you consider my stepmother to be?'

'Mrs Slade was also present?'

'There's no reason to be so surprised. Step-relationships don't have to be all snarls. She and I understand each other very well.'

'When did she leave?'

'I don't remember saying that she did.'

'Did she?'

'Only to go to bed.'

'Which was when?'

'Some time after midnight.'

'When did Mr Rees leave?'

'Then.'

'Is Mrs Slade at home now?'

'She was shortly before you arrived. I can't answer more accurately than that.'

'Would you please find out if she is still at home.'

'Juan will tell you. The bell's to the right of the fireplace.'

Metcalf was damned if he was going to play the part of a servant. He nodded at Tyler. Tyler, his expression indicating nothing in particular, stood, crossed to the fireplace and rang the bell at the side of the ornately carved marble surround.

Juan, dressed in white coat and striped trousers, entered.

'Is Mrs Slade in?' Calvin asked.

'Yes, Mr Calvin. In conservatory,' Juan answered, making a hash of the last word.

'Tell her that if she's not too busy, there are two local detectives who'd like a word with her.'

Juan left.

'What did you do that Friday evening?' Metcalf asked.

'Nothing unusual.'

'What do you consider usual?'

'Dinner, a game or two of Trivial Pursuit, a tape.'

'Can you remember what the tape was?'

'*Seven Brides For Seven Brothers.*'

'Did Mrs Slade watch it with you?'

'It was she who chose it, I suspect because of the barn dance. She is firmly of the opinion that had she not married my father, she would have become a very successful dancer.'

They waited, not trying to make polite conversation.

Fenella entered. Metcalf and Tyler immediately rose to their feet, Calvin remained sprawled out in the armchair. 'They're detectives,' Calvin said, in a bored, throwaway tone. 'They're asking questions about Friday before last. It seems they . . .'

'It'll be best if I explain,' interrupted Metcalf. He faced her. 'I'm sorry to bother you, but we'd be grateful for your help.' He'd seen photographs of her in papers and magazines, but none had provided a true impression. She was one of the most immediately attractive women he had met. Her looks were enhanced by cool taste – she wore little make-up, her dress was simple, even if that simplicity had been expensive, and apart from engagement and wedding rings she wore only one small piece of jewellery – yet, paradoxically, she possessed the underlying hint of sexuality that had any man with red blood wondering if she was as good at bedroom gymnastics as instinct suggested.

She went over to the nearest free chair and sat; she crossed her legs, tugged down the hem of her skirt. It was equally possible to view her actions as those of a demure woman or one who knew how subtly to hold a man's attention.

Metcalf said: 'We're making certain inquiries in the course of which it has become necessary to determine where certain people were on the night of the ninth – that's the Friday before last. Would you be kind enough to tell us where you were then?'

She considered the question for a while, then said, in her carefully modulated voice: 'Why do you want to know?'

'Because you may be able to confirm what we've just been told.'

'By Calvin?'

'That is correct.'

'I'll have to check in my diary because I've such a terrible memory. Would you like me to go upstairs to fetch it?'

'Yes, please.'

She stood, crossed to the door. Metcalf found himself watching her, noticing how her frock momentarily drew tight against each buttock in turn. He hastily looked away, to meet Calvin's sarcastic scorn.

When she returned, she held a small, leatherbound book in one hand. She sat, opened the diary, turned back several pages. 'I came back at four. Calvin was here and Timothy turned up a bit later on. We had dinner, only a light meal, of course, because that was Juan and Dolores's half day.'

'And after the meal?'

'We played Trivial Pursuit.' She smiled. 'I didn't win a game. I'm not very clever when it comes to that sort of thing.'

'Don't belittle yourself,' said Calvin. 'You'd have won

the last one if only you'd remembered that nothing exceeds like success.'

Metcalf was certain that that was a misquote, but infuriatingly couldn't silently correct it. 'What happened after you finished playing?'

'We watched *Seven Brides For Seven Brothers*.'

'Can you remember what the time was when Mr Rees left here?'

She shrugged her shoulders.

'Ten o'clock?'

'Much later than that. It certainly was after midnight, but I've no idea exactly when.'

Metcalf stood. 'Thank you for your help.' He took one pace towards the door, then stopped. 'By the way, Mr Slade, was your Bentley on the road that night?'

'Since I was here all evening, the answer has to be in the negative, doesn't it?'

'So it wasn't parked in front of Jenton Coldstores?'

'No, it wasn't.'

'Someone's old Bentley was. There can't be many of them around, so I'm sure we'll find out whose it was.'

'When you do, tell the owner to join the club if he isn't already a member.'

Metcalf led the way through the lofty hall and out to the CID Escort. As Tyler drove round the central flowerbed, he said: 'It's his kind that gives money a bad name.'

21

'Damn!' said the chief constable. A product of the old school, that was the strongest expletive he allowed himself in the hearing of his secretary.

'Shall I tell him you're in conference?' she suggested.

'He'll only ring back and I'd rather get it over and done with . . . You'll have to put him through.' He drummed his fingers on the desk. He wondered why, in the face of a rising crime rate, an over-the-top budget, a force depleted by an above average rate of sickness, and a daughter who'd become entangled with a long-haired, guitar-playing student who didn't think that grass grew on lawns, he had had to be saddled with a chairman of the Police Authority who thought Yorkshire bluntness was an asset?

'Have you read the papers?' was Armstrong's greeting.

'I've skimmed through *The Times*. My secretary's marked items in other papers which are of interest.'

'Then you'll have seen it?'

'I imagine you're referring to the article about Burrell?'

'Aye.'

'My ACC tells me it's no more accurate than usual.'

'Was he or wasn't he beaten up and tortured?'

'The medical evidence supports his claim that he was.'

'By vigilantes?'

'That's possible.'

'The umpteenth incident this month.'

'In the past four weeks, the precise number, including this, is three.'

'Which is three too many.'

'I certainly can't argue with that.'

'Do you know what the definition of a vigilante is? A self-appointed maintainer of order in an imperfectly organized community. These vigilantes are telling everyone that law and order in this county is hopelessly organized.'

'I would cross swords with that conclusion.'

'Would you? What's happening to the crime figures?'

'Unfortunately, there has been a slight increase . . .'

'Which way is the clear-up rate heading?'

'It's true there has been a slight decrease, but that's due . . .'

'I talk to the man in the street, he says you've lost the battle and that's why you're encouraging the vigilantes to do your job for you.'

'That is a monstrous accusation.'

'Then why haven't you arrested a single vigilante?'

'Such cases almost always present special difficulties. Sympathy lies with the vigilantes and so people are very reluctant to testify against them.'

'Have your blokes conducted any sort of an investigation to find out who did the torturing?'

'Of course.'

'But without result.'

'My ACC assures me we can be certain we have identified the two men responsible.'

'So you've arrested them?'

'No.'

'Why not?'

'They have an alibi. In such circumstances, the CPS would never warrant their arrest.'

'If they're guilty, the alibi's a fake.'

'Of course.'

'It's not occurred to any of you to prove that? I'll tell you straight from the shoulder. I reckon the man in the street knows a thing or two.'

*   *   *

141

The assistant chief constable (Crime) said: 'He's steaming, Harry; boiler's at danger pressure.'

'Didn't you explain . . . ?' began the detective chief superintendent.

'He knows the facts. But the chairman of the Police Authority is riding on his shoulders. How certain are you that the assailants have been correctly identified?'

'The divisional DI says there can't be a shadow of doubt.'

'That's Metcalf, isn't it? A good man, if I remember his flimsies.'

'Came a cropper on the Tyrell case, but that was over-enthusiasm, not incompetence. His only other problem is a lack of tact.'

'Why hasn't he broken the alibis?'

'Mrs Slade is providing them so it's a case of money, position, and power. She can't be pressured as if she were Mrs Brown from Camden Town. On top of that, Metcalf's short-handed and can't afford to spend over-much time on any one case.'

'From now on he can. Whatever it takes, that alibi has to be broken and the two men brought to trial so that the message goes out loud and clear that we're not in the business of encouraging vigilantes.'

Metcalf turned away from the window, crossed to the desk, sat. 'You're certain?'

'As certain as I can be in the circumstances,' Grey replied. 'Rees appeared really shocked when I said Burrell had been tortured. And that squares with Burrell's evidence that one man went outside before the other actually applied the prod and then kicked him. My guess is that Rees thought they were only going to use the threat of force to try to make Burrell confess.'

'If that's right, he's suddenly discovered he's in something very much nastier than he reckoned on. Which should leave him nervous and ready, if not eager, to come clean. Moving on, how do we tackle Mrs Slade?'

'With kid gloves.'

Metcalf rubbed his chin. 'Servants can be a good source of information. She said it was their half day. I'll bet a fortune she never does any washing-up, so they may be able to say if there were signs of three people having had dinner. What's more, they may know if there are any ski-masks and suits, an electrical prod and a gun still around. The envelope was typewritten, so we need examples of the type of any machine in the house. Neighbours must be questioned to find out if any of 'em heard the old banger drive away during the time Calvin claims to have been home.'

'All that's going to call for heavy manpower,' Grey said.

'So find it. I've had the DCS on the phone for half an hour, demanding results. If we don't get something fast, he'll be down to take charge.'

Christine entered Timothy's bedroom, shut the door. 'There are two more detectives who want to talk to you and one of them's a detective inspector. You're in some sort of real trouble, aren't you?'

'It'll just be more questions . . .'

'Tim, I must know so that I can help.'

After a while, he said: 'They seem convinced Calvin and I were responsible for torturing Burrell.'

'Oh, my God! You said the other day they thought . . . I told myself you couldn't have been so stupid as to let Calvin lead you into something that terrible.'

'I didn't.'

'You promise me?'

He prevaricated. 'We were at his place all evening. Mrs Slade has told the police that.'

Her relief was immediate. 'Then why are they wasting their time coming back here?'

'They'll just be checking up on something or other. Don't worry, it can't be serious.'

She said nothing more as she watched him leave.

At the foot of the stairs, he paused. Over the phone, Calvin had said the police had swallowed the alibi, hook, line, and sinker because Fenella had backed them up all the way . . . He took a deep breath, went through to the sitting room.

Metcalf, his manner briskly pleasant, said: 'I thought it only fair to come here and personally explain something . . . Why don't you sit down?'

Timothy sat and only then thought that Metcalf, who had remained standing, had perhaps been employing simple psychology to impose a sense of authority. He stood, went over to one of the small tables, rearranged some magazines. 'My mother has a thing about tidiness . . . Won't you sit?'

They all sat. Fifteen-all, Timothy thought, gaining confidence from the unspoken – perhaps imaginary – conflict.

'Before I say anything, would you like to alter the evidence you gave my detective sergeant?'

'I've no reason to.'

'Very well . . . I understand you're reading law?'

'Yes.'

'Then you will know that if two persons set out to commit a crime and it is agreed that force may be used in the commission of it, both are equally guilty if this force is inflicted by only one of them?'

'Yes.'

'Broadly speaking, that concept holds good where there is no definite agreement to use force, but the circumstances are such that any reasonable person would appreciate that the need for it will be likely. Where there is room for doubt is when the first man can be certain force will be employed, but the circumstances are not sufficiently clear cut for the second man, as a reasonable person, to realize this. In most such cases, the courts will accept that the second man's guilt is less than his companion's even though he willingly and knowingly set out to commit a crime. In practical terms, this acceptance can mean the difference between a light and a heavy sentence. You understand what I'm saying?'

'I understand the what, but not the why.'

'I am quite certain that you have the intelligence to understand precisely why . . . Having questioned you, my detective sergeant was convinced you had had no idea that Burrell had suffered torture and then been brutally kicked. Were you shocked to learn that this was so?'

'Of course I was.'

'Because it had been agreed that only the threat of physical harm should be employed; because you were well aware that if Burrell confessed but could prove his confession was extracted by force it would be inadmissible?'

'Because any normal person would be shocked.'

'The difference between a light sentence and a heavy one can mean the difference between a salvaged life and a ruined one.'

'Calvin and I were at his house all that evening.'

Metcalf said to Tyler: 'There are some you can help and some you can't.' He stood.

As the front door closed on the two detectives, Christine hurried into the hall. 'What did they want?'

'They asked some questions, I answered them.'

'About Burrell?'

'Yes.'

'And they're satisfied?'

'No handcuffs.'

After a moment, she said: 'There's something I don't understand. If Mrs Slade told the police you and Calvin were with her all evening, how can they go on worrying you when they know it couldn't have been anything to do with you?'

'I asked them that precise question. They didn't have an answer. Maybe they're just trying to give the impression that they aren't at a complete loss.'

As he drove along the road, Tyler said: 'Some people can be thicker than a barn door.'

'Thick or hidebound?'

'How d'you mean, sir?'

'You need to remember his milieu – very different from

145

that of our usual customer. He's public school – stands out a mile, despite the semi-detached. There's one inflexible rule in all those places – never, never sneak.'

Tyler thought about that. 'Sounds like the villains.'

'That's right. So on second thoughts, maybe after all the two milieus have something in common.'

22

'It's enough to make one join a nunnery,' Naylor said as he pulled out and overtook a van. 'Burrell rapes a woman at knife-point, but gets away with it because we're not allowed the time and manpower to do our damnedest to prove the alibi a fake; Slade and Rees put the boot in and we're told to break their alibi whatever the cost. Where's the logic?'

'If you're looking for logic,' said Grey, 'you've a bloody long search ahead of you.'

'Why doesn't the Guv'nor let this slide?'

'Because his orders have come down from on high.'

'Shall I tell you something?'

'I'd rather you didn't.'

'I'm hoping these Portuguese don't know a damn thing.'

'In that case, I'll do all the talking. And just to keep you with it, they're Filipino.'

'So where's the difference?'

'Set sail for Lisbon and you'll discover.'

A mile along the lane, they turned into the oak-lined drive of Franklin Manor. As the full size of the Carolean house became visible, Naylor whistled. 'How the other half lives!'

'"Bow, bow, ye lower middle classes!"'

'Like bloody hell!'

'No need to burst a blood vessel. That wasn't an order, but a quote from *Iolanthe*.'

'I never could stand that sort of stuff.'

'I'm not surprised. Slow down so as I can have a bit

147

more of a think ... We want to chat 'em up without being interrupted, so it'll be best if we go round to the tradesmen's entrance ... Should have thought of that before and used the other approach.'

They rounded the raised flowerbed and drove down a gravel path that took them along the east side of the house to the large courtyard.

Two doors were visible. Naylor rang the bell at the side of the nearer one. When Juan Estaur opened it, he introduced himself.

'Mr Slade, out; Mrs Slade, out; Mr Calvin out. All out.'

Grey said in a friendly tone: 'It's you and your wife we'd like a chat with; nothing serious. So perhaps we could come in?'

Estaur, very uneasy, led the way past the game larder and a storeroom, through the large kitchen that appeared to be equipped with every type of electrical gadget on the market, and into a room that was furnished adequately, but with odd pieces.

'Is your wife here?' Grey asked.

He nodded.

'We'd like to talk to her as well.'

He left.

'Not exactly a chatterbox,' said Naylor, as he sat.

'Perhaps the police his way are a lot rougher than us.'

Estaur returned, accompanied by his wife. As slightly built as he, the roughened skin of her heavily-lined face suggested that in her youth she had spent much time working in harsh sunshine.

Grey explained that all they wanted was to check up on a few facts and his manner gradually put them more at their ease. Did they remember the ninth, the Friday before last?

They spoke to each other in rapid Spanish, then Estaur said: 'We have holiday.'

'So when did you leave the house?'

'We go at the twelve. See friends.'

'You didn't serve lunch?'

148

'Mr Calvin, gone; Mrs Slade, gone; Mr Slade, gone.'

'Then you wouldn't know when Mrs Slade returned?'

'She with friend.'

'Where was Calvin Slade?'

'Not know.'

'When did you return here?'

'It was late.'

'Can you say how late?'

'It was one of the morning.'

'Were the family back?'

'No understand.'

Grey rephrased the question.

Estaur explained at length, helped or hindered by his wife – it was not quite certain which – that their duties normally ceased after dinner had been served and cleared. Then they retired to their quarters. The family always locked the front of the house and secured the alarms and consequently it was normally impossible for them to know who was in the house late at night.

'When it's your half day and the family get their own meal, do they clear the table afterwards?'

Sometimes they did; mostly, they didn't.

'Was it cleared that Friday?'

They conferred. They thought the table had been cleared.

'So what happened to all the dirty cutlery, plates, and glasses?'

They couldn't remember. Perhaps they'd been stacked in the washing-up machine; the family sometimes did that rather than leaving things on the table.

'Was the machine pretty full on the Saturday morning?'

They couldn't remember that either.

'Calvin Slade says he's a very keen skier.'

They accepted this without any visible emotion.

'Does he have a lot of ski clothes – you know, smart ski-suits and those masks with funny designs?'

They'd never seen any.

Grey swung the conversation round to a general

discussion of the delights of living in a large and beautiful house in the countryside. Of course, he added, there was a downside – security became very difficult. The Estaurs had said that there was an alarm system but probably the Slades had a mobile phone in case the telephone wires were cut? And also some form of personal defence? A handgun maybe? A stungun maybe?

Dolores told them, showing a sense of humour which was seldom evident from her expression, about the thing the Señor had brought back from America for the Señora. Tiny, but when the Señora had shown it to her and pressed the button, lightning had flashed from one prong to the other; and when she had unwisely put a finger too close, it had felt like the time when she'd been young and had put her finger in a saucepan of jam, not knowing it had just come off the wood fire . . .

Grey said they ought to be going. But there was one last question. Had they any idea where Mrs Slade had gone that Friday?

They conferred. 'Not knowing,' Estaur said. "Perhaps same person when Mr Slade out other times.'

'And who would that be?'

'Señora Lawson,' she said.

'Do you know where she lives?'

Estaur answered. 'Only know telephone if Mr Slade want speak.'

'Perhaps you'll give me the number you have to ring?'

He left, to return with a slip of paper on which he'd written.

As they passed through the second gateway, in sharp contrast to the elaborate main one, Naylor said: 'Mrs Slade's getting it on the side.'

'Don't you ever think of anything else?' Grey said wearily.

'Look, she's a whole lot younger than her husband.'

'And in your book, that's a guarantee of adultery?'

'He's also big business, so even when he's home he's

probably more interested in who to do down than in doing her. She'll be looking for some fun.'

'So your next suggestion is that Mrs Lawson and her make a perfect couple?'

'Or the Lawson woman is providing her with cover. Remember how the servants have to phone if her old man starts wanting to chat with her?'

'That couldn't be just so that she can return home to greet hubby as he arrives? I'd hate to hear your thoughts on Jonathan and David ... Get on the blower and ask someone to find out the address which corresponds with this telephone number.'

They were given an address in Retlington, a village that had escaped almost all development and still consisted of no more than a dozen houses or bungalows and one pub. Acorn Farm lay less than a quarter of a mile from the crossroads. It was a typical seventeenth-century farm-house with peg-tile roof, which on the south side sloped down to within a few feet of the ground, variegated bricks, and beamed ceilings which posed a threat to anyone taller than five feet nine.

Rowena Lawson, in her early thirties, was a woman of warmth rather than beauty, who dressed for her own comfort and not for style. She answered their questions without hesitation. Fenella Slade was an old friend and quite often visited her for the day, or part of the day; on the Friday in question, she'd been there from midday to around four.

'Probably not lesbians,' said Grey, as they drove out on to the lane. 'You must feel real disappointed.'

'Did you notice something, Sarge? She never once wanted to know why we were asking the questions. That's odd.'

'Don't you ever have a nice thought?'

Metcalf replaced the receiver. The detective chief super-intendent was not a subtle man. If the alibi was a fake, an efficient detective inspector would quickly uncover the evidence to prove this and by doing so would persuade his seniors that his part in the Tyrell case should be forgotten. On the other hand, an inefficient detective inspector could expect a second black mark on his flimsies and that must ensure an early retirement . . .

He used the internal phone to call Grey into his room. 'Were Slade and Rees the two vigilantes?'

'Yes, sir.'

'No doubts?'

'None.'

'Their alibi's a fake?'

'It has to be.'

'Then why the goddamn hell can't we prove that it is? Is there something we're all missing?'

It was obvious that this was to be an informal session. Grey brought his pipe from his pocket. 'Is it all right if I smoke?'

'The window's open.'

Humour didn't improve with rank. 'They went for Burrell because they knew he'd raped Miss Hurst. There's motive, opportunity, and just about enough evidence to get them to court . . . Except for the alibi.'

'That's one bloody big exception.'

He struck a match, drew on the pipe until it was well alight. 'Would it do any good to question Mrs Slade again?'

'Almost certainly not. But for lack of any other course . . . Mrs Lawson was certain Mrs Slade left her place at around four?'

'That's what she said.'

'It backs up Mrs Slade's evidence.'

'It's significant that Slade and Rees chose a Friday – that's the Filipinos' half day.'

'It's significant to you and me, but offer that to a court and defence counsel would choke laughing.'

'Then it looks as if we're at the end of the road.'

'Not my road. Think of something. Anything. Let your mind loose.'

The pipe had gone out. About to strike another match,

Grey lowered his right hand. 'There could just be one possibility. It's a real long shot.'

'I don't give a damn if it's from here to there.'

'Naylor reckons Mrs Slade is having it off with someone; either with Mrs Lawson, or she's using Mrs Lawson as a cover in case hubby comes back unexpectedly.'

'Why's he think that?'

'Basically, because she's considerably younger than the husband, who's away much of the time; when it comes to women, Fred's a cliché.'

'So we forget the idea?'

'There's just one point. Mrs Lawson never once asked us why we put the questions about Mrs Slade.'

'Which normally one would have expected her to . . . How do you place Mrs Lawson?'

'Thoroughly respectable. Probably does good work in the parish.'

'Then she might resent having to cover if Mrs Slade is screwing around.'

Mrs Lawson looked from Metcalf to Grey, unable to conceal her unease. 'I've answered those questions before.'

'Indeed,' said Metcalf, sitting to the right of the large inglenook fireplace. 'But I'm wondering if you understand the significance of your answers?'

'I don't follow that.'

Grey had been right, he thought. She was the epitome of respectability – though not in any snide sense – and her standards would always be high. So if Fenella Slade had been asking her to act as a cover, the friendship must have been stretched to the limit. It shouldn't be difficult to stretch it that little bit further. 'Mrs Lawson, may I ask you to treat with the utmost confidence what I tell you?'

'You may.'

'We are investigating a case in which two men brutally assaulted and tortured a third.'

'What a terrible world it seems to have become,' she said bitterly.

'And the only way of stopping it becoming worse, let alone rolling the violence back, is to make certain that those who consider committing it understand that if they do so, they will probably suffer condign punishment. And the way in which we, the police, can help to bring that about is to increase our rate of successful arrests in high-profile cases which receive considerable publicity. If we can arrest the two who committed this assault and torture, we shall be doing just that . . . I think you can help us.'

'How?'

'By telling us the truth, even if it breaches the confidence of friendship.'

She stared for a long time through the small, slightly arched leaded window. Then she said, without facing him: 'What exactly do you want to know?'

'When did Mrs Slade leave this house?'

'Immediately after lunch; about two o'clock.'

'Did she return home?'

'No.'

'Do you know where she went?'

'All I have is a telephone number which I ring if I need to speak to her.'

'Because Mr Slade has unexpectedly returned home and is wondering where she is?'

After a while, she nodded.

'Will you give me that number, please?'

She left the room, automatically ducking under the lintel to go into the hall. When she returned, she handed Metcalf a small square of paper.

'Thank you,' he said.

'You have made me despise myself.'

'That's the last thing you should do, Mrs Lawson. In our work, time and again we meet people who have to decide either to do something which is wrong but easy, or right, but difficult. It is only the honest and the strong who choose the latter course.'

He'd really sounded as if he'd meant that, Grey thought,

completely misjudging the sincerity with which the detective inspector had spoken.

Depending on definition, Retford Cross was either a large village or a small town. Along the main street, which ran from east to west, were many shops that sold quality rather than quantity, a sure indication of the fact that the area was a wealthy one.

Geoffrey Tierson's house was on the northern outskirts, overlooking the first fields. A large, square, red brick building, it lacked any character; he provided that. He had an unkempt red beard which matched his unkempt, red, curly hair; his heavy features spoke unmistakably of earthy appetites; his clothes would have been rejected by a church bazaar; his manner was loud and crude. Many were reluctant to admit that he was a very talented painter.

'Why no booze? Because of all that crap about not drinking on duty? Jeeze, if I had to be TT whilst working, I wouldn't bloody work.' He crossed to the array of bottles on the beautiful Georgian sideboard, his flip-flops slapping against his soles.

'How long have you known Mrs Slade?' Metcalf asked.

'Since her old man commissioned me to paint her portrait.' He poured out a large whisky, added a splash of soda. He flip-flopped his way back to the nearest chair, sat, drank, belched.

'Have you finished it?'

'Months ago.'

'Seen her since then?'

'Maybe, maybe not.'

'Was she here on Friday, the ninth?'

'What's it to you?'

'I've explained.'

'And if I don't give shit for your explanation?'

'I'm trying to conduct the investigation as discreetly as possible. Should you have formed a close friendship with Mrs Slade and as a result of that she was here on the ninth, but that fact proves to be of no direct concern to us, we shall forget it. On the other hand, if we have to make much wider inquiries to establish the truth, it's more than probable that Mr Slade will learn this. He will be far less ready to forget. Even in this day and age, the rich can be extraordinarily and successfully vindictive.'

Tierson drank heavily. 'All right, she was here.'

'Until when?'

'Eleven, twelve. She's bloody insatiable.'

Metcalf faced Fenella across the green room; he and Grey stood by the Steinway, which was kept in perfect tune but never played, she in front of the small Turner. 'Mrs Slade, you obviously don't understand the situation. You do not have the option of deciding whether to give evidence; if it becomes necessary, you will be subpoenaed to do so.'

'You bastards!'

'We're merely doing our job.'

'And loving every minute of shoving your snouts into other people's lives.'

'Were you at the home of Mr Tierson on the afternoon and evening of the ninth?'

She hesitated.

'If you admit it now, that fact may well never have to be aired in court. If you do not, we shall certainly have to call both you and Mr Tierson to testify.'

'All right, I was with him,' she shouted. 'And now d'you want a minute-by-minute description, so you can get your cheap little thrills?'

23

Not even the car crash had convinced Rees that life preferred tragedy to comedy. 'Circumstantial evidence isn't ever very strong, is it?'

Evans, in years middle age, in experience old, replied: 'I'm not trying to be clever, Nick, but it all depends on the circumstances.' Their friendship stretched back over thirty years, which made him wish that Rees had decided to go to another solicitor.

'It could easily not have been a Bentley outside the coldstore.'

'I understand that the witness who saw it is an enthusiast and identifies it very precisely.'

'All right. But how many of them are on the roads?'

'I know a keen Bentley man and he's given me some figures.' Evans searched amongst some papers on his desk. 'Only six hundred and sixty-five four and a half litre Bentleys were built, of which roughly three hundred and fifty-six are known still to exist.'

'That doesn't stop this one being owned by someone other than Calvin.'

'Nick, if that were the only evidence against them, it would hold very little water. A jury would accept the possibility, or probability, of its belonging to someone else. But even here, the surrounding circumstances matter. The store is owned by his father's company. He worked there. How could an unknown driver have gained access to the yard without disturbing padlock or chain? Why should he have done so? Why should he have handled the keys of one of the vans unless to use it on the road?

'But it's not a piece of evidence in isolation. It's one strand of many. And when all the strands are woven together, it must add considerable strength to the whole.'

Rees rubbed the side of his nose, a habit of his when worried. 'Tim and Calvin can't prove they were at Franklin Manor all evening, but that doesn't prove they weren't.'

'Of course not. But the fact that no one can vouch for their presence there at the relevant times means the jury will find it easy to consider the possibility that they weren't.'

'You're saying . . . You're saying that the case against them is strong?'

'They wouldn't have been arrested and charged if it were not.' Evans wondered if Rees really did believe in the innocence of his son? 'Tim now needs as a matter of urgency to consider the question of Legal Aid and who is to handle his case.'

'You are.'

'I'm afraid I don't belong to the scheme.'

'That'll have to go by the board.'

'Nick, I've tried to explain, my forte is civil law.'

'But you'll fight really hard because you know him personally.'

'That can easily be a minus, not a plus; emotion can affect judgement.'

'Not with you. Handle it, please?'

Against his will, he nodded.

'You'll get hold of a top barrister. How much will that cost?'

'A good QC will expect his brief to be marked at several hundred guineas; with refreshers at two-thirds. On top of that, there's his junior, the preliminary work, and the consultations. You'll be looking at a bill of several thousands.' Evans knew what this must mean to Rees and the new life he had slowly and so laboriously built up after the accident. 'My advice remains, use the scheme to find a solicitor who specializes in criminal law . . .'

'It has to be you. And I want you to brief a really good man.'

It was an illogical attitude, yet Evans had learned how stress so often made people illogical. 'There is an alternative. Slade's bound to brief the best QC that money can buy. There's no reason why he shouldn't represent both Tim and Calvin.'

'Christine and I have never been happy about the friendship. I should dislike asking a favour of the family.'

'You don't think that perhaps this is a time to put personal feelings to one side?'

'Practicalities before prejudices and principles?'

'The cost of the law has ruined many more men of principles than practicalities.'

'If the car's free,' Timothy said, 'I'll run over now and have a word with Calvin.'

'That's a good idea,' Rees replied.

'I'm sure he'll agree.'

'He should do,' snapped Christine. 'After all . . .' She stopped as she caught the look her husband gave her.

They were trying so hard, Timothy thought miserably; trying not to show that they simply couldn't understand how he'd allowed himself to be so disastrously influenced by Calvin. If only Calvin hadn't been such a fool as actually to use torture when the fear of it appeared to be insufficient . . . If only. The two most dangerous words in the English language. 'Are the keys in the car?'

'I'm afraid so — left them there when I got back. Broke my own rule.' Rees tried, and failed, to sound amusedly self-condemnatory.

Timothy left and went out to the Renault, settled behind the wheel. The engine proved even more reluctant than usual to fire. A couple of days ago, the mechanic at the garage had said that the underbody rust was so serious it would hardly be worth stripping down the engine as previously suggested and it was high time the car was pensioned off. Yet now there could be no chance that his parents could afford even a cheap replacement.

When he turned off the lane, passed through the elaborate gateway, and started up the oak-lined drive, he experienced for the first time a hatred of the Slades' wealth. It was a hatred based not on a suddenly uncovered jealousy, but on the certainty that it was this wealth which, by convincing Calvin that he was above the law, had brought about the present disaster; that it was going to cushion Calvin's family whilst his own would be financially devastated; that it was forcing him now to beg; that it had bought his friendship, without his ever allowing himself to accept that fact . . .

He parked by the raised flowerbed, crossed to the portico and rang the bell. Estaur said that Mr Calvin was not in, but Mr Slade was. He showed Timothy into the green room.

Slade entered. Although only five feet eight tall, few ever thought of him as a small man – he possessed in large measure the presence which was the badge of those in high places or of great wealth. 'Calvin's not here.'

'So Juan said . . .'

'Then what do you want?'

Even experience had not prepared Timothy for this degree of antagonistic abruptness. 'To have a word with you, if I may?'

'What about?'

'You know the preliminary hearing is coming up . . .'

'So?'

'After that there'll be the trial. My solicitor says I need to be represented by a first-class barrister; silk, if possible.'

'It should hardly need a solicitor to tell you that.'

'The thing is . . . a really good barrister is very expensive. So we were wondering . . . Who's representing Calvin?'

'Sir Arnold Baxter.'

'He has a tremendous name.'

160

'That is why we are employing him.'

It was in style for Slade to say he was 'employing' the most eminent QC in criminal work. Timothy said, in a rush of words: 'We were wondering if Sir Arnold could represent me as well?'

'Very inadvisable. Is that all?'

'Mr Slade, since Calvin and I are being charged together . . .'

'You will make your own arrangements.' Slade turned and left.

Timothy felt like the starving beggar contemptuously refused a crust of bread at the castle gate.

24

'Members of the jury,' said Crocker-Smith, a leading counsel tipped for elevation to the Bench, 'in this opening speech it is my duty to set before you those facts which the prosecution will prove in court . . .' He had a mellifluous voice and the calm, slightly elevated, slightly disengaged manner of a man who had risen above human failings to view the world in pure truth.

'. . . Almost every crime has a motive and in this case the motive is the strong part of the crime. It will, therefore, be necessary to make explicit what that motive was and in order to do so I shall have to make reference to another criminal act, to wit, an act of rape. Whenever such reference is made I will, with his Lordship's permission, refer to the victim as Miss X.'

The judge looked over his half moon glasses at the benches reserved for the very many reporters who were present. 'I direct you that the victim is not to be named, nor are any details to be written or spoken which might lead to her identification.' He settled back in his gold-embossed, leather-upholstered chair. He had austere features, but was not a man of austere beliefs. 'Please continue, Mr Crocker-Smith.'

'Thank you, my Lord . . . Members of the jury, Miss X, a close friend of both accused, was one night savagely raped in the garden of her home. In the course of the subsequent investigation, the police identified a possible suspect and it became clear to Miss X, from the questions put to her, that this was Mr Burrell, the victim in this case, who had been working as an electrician in her home earlier on the day of the rape. It thus happened, in the natural course of events, that both the accused became aware of the fact that initially the police suspected Mr Burrell.

'Further inquiries then established the fact that Mr Burrell had an unshakable alibi, provided by Mr Fossen and Mr Daniels, who will be called to testify that he was with them throughout the evening of the rape. You must understand that they are being called not to prove his innocence – since that is beyond doubt – but to prove that anyone who knew the nature of their evidence must, if of a reasonable mind, have accepted Mr Burrell's innocence. Conversely, that to reject it demonstrates such an unreasonable state of mind that there can be no shred of sympathy for such rejection.'

Crocker-Smith flicked the tails of his wig clear of the wing collar, readjusted the set of his gown with a quick shrug of the shoulders. He briefly looked down at his notes. 'Members of the jury, you will all be conversant with the expression "vigilante". No doubt the word provides each of you with a slightly different mental picture and there may even be amongst you someone who conceives a vigilante to be a man who provides justice where the law cannot or will not. Such a picture could not be more incorrect. A vigilante is someone who ignores all evidence, spurns all rules, and arrogantly appoints himself judge, jury and executioner. A vigilante is as much a criminal as he believes his victim to be; an even greater one when his victim is innocent.

'It is the prosecution's contention that the accused in this case convinced themselves that Burrell was guilty of the rape of Miss X despite the police's determination that he could not have been; that they decided to terrify and to torture him into making a false confession; that having learned from the investigation how any police inquiry would be conducted, they planned their crime in a way that they hoped and believed would prevent their being charged . . .

There was a cafeteria for the public, a part of which was reserved for witnesses.The food, it had been said, was like the law – it went back a long time.

'Can't he understand?' said Rees bitterly, as he put down his fork. 'He talks as if it was all remote, sanitized, impersonal. But when Tim saw her in hospital, his emotions were bruised raw.'

'I'm afraid the law seldom makes allowances for emotions,' Evans said.

'I hope to God Creedon understands more about them than the law does, then.'

'You can rely on that. He's a good man.'

'But without very much experience.'

'I've known barristers with thirty years' experience who weren't up to anything but routine work. He's smart, sharp, a real fighter.'

'And he needs to be all of that?'

'I'm afraid so.'

Timothy's housemaster had often said that an intelligent man should never hesitate to seek out a fresh experience, provided it was not illegal or immoral. Which proved how stupid schoolmasters could be. Who but an idiot would seek out the fresh experience of being locked up during the lunch recession in a cell that smelled of stale urine and despair . . .

He knew a desperate longing for the nightmare to end; and a desperate fear of the moment when it would.

As they stepped out of the car, Christine opened the front door. 'Well?'

'The prosecution's only just completed its opening speech,' replied Rees. 'They must be paying him by the word.'

164

She drew Timothy to her and hugged him as she had not done in years.

Much later, when they were in bed, she said to her husband: 'What does Andrew think?'

'He's hopeful.'

'Thank God for that!'

It was not often that he lied to her.

Both in appearance and manner, Baxter was the antithesis to Crocker-Smith. Short, plump, with a ready, toothy smile, he cultivated a degree of untidiness to suggest the typical, down-to-earth family man; a man of the people, sharing their triumphs and their tragedies, able to smile at the former and sympathize with the latter.

He faced the witness box, his silk gown looking crumpled, his wig in need of a shampoo. 'WPC Carmichael, in the course of your duties, did you visit Miss X in hospital?'

'Yes, sir,' she answered. 'On three occasions.'

'Did you meet either of the defendants there?'

'Once. I had been detailed to see if Miss X could provide more information than she had been able to do up to then. On my arrival, Mr Rees was present.'

'Will you describe the circumstances, please?'

'He was sitting on the bed, holding her hand.'

'Did you at any time meet Mr Slade at the hospital?'

'No, sir.'

'Did Miss X mention whether Mr Slade had ever visited her there?'

Crocker-Smith rose. 'My Lord, my learned friend really can't expect that question to be allowed.'

'I expect he would agree with you,' replied the judge, with light irony.

Crocker-Smith sat. Baxter, cheerfully certain the jury had grasped the point even if they were not yet aware of that fact, said: 'Did you visit Miss X at her home after she was discharged from hospital?'

'Yes, sir, on at least two occasions; it may have been

three, but I'd have to consult my notebook to be certain.'

'I don't think that that is necessary. Whilst you were there, was Mr Slade at any time present?'

'No, sir.'

'Was Mr Rees?'

'Yes, sir.'

'Thank you.' He sat.

'No questions,' said Creedon.

'No further questions,' said Crocker-Smith, hardly bothering to rise.

Evans returned from the bar with three glasses on a small tray, put the glasses down on the table, sat. He drank. 'Creedon suggested it would be a good idea if I had a word with you.'

Rees and Timothy waited, neither of them drinking.

'Tim, in your studies have you come across the law relating to two persons who jointly commit a crime and their respective degrees of guilt?'

'Yes,' Timothy replied.

'Do you understand the subtleties of it?'

'I think so. In any case, the police made the situation very clear.'

'They did?' Evans showed surprise, then concern. 'When was this?'

'One of the interviews before they arrested me.'

'Were they offering you a possible escape route?'

'Provided I dumped Calvin in the mire.'

'Blast!'

'What's the significance of all this?' Rees asked.

'Tim was offered a legitimate way of escaping the most severe penalties by admitting his guilt, but disclaiming any knowledge that actual, physical assault was intended. Since the average man would imagine that Timothy would have jumped at that offer if in a position to do so, the fact that he didn't will suggest he wasn't in such a position . . . Did anything strike either of you about Baxter's cross-examination of the police witnesses?'

Rees said: 'Only that he was a lot less pugnacious than I'd expected.'

'Exactly. And it's because of his cross-examinations that Creedon asked me to speak to you. On the face of things, much of it was irrelevant. Repeatedly, he asked how often Timothy or Calvin had been seen with Miss Hurst and clearly that can have had no direct bearing on whether either or both of them assaulted Burrell. But it may very well indicate the course of Baxter's future handling of the case ... I suppose you realize just how strong is the prosecution's evidence?'

After a moment, Rees, carefully not looking at Timothy, said: 'Yes.'

'So strong that it has to be realistic to consider what the penalties are likely to be?'

There was no answer. Timothy tried to control his expression.

'Baxter's cross-examinations of the police witnesses suggests that Calvin has decided to take the path which you, Timothy, refused – in other words, at the last moment to change his plea to guilty and then to testify that the original idea was yours, that he'd no idea you intended to use actual force, and that he took no part in the use of force because he was outside the house when Burrell was tortured and repeatedly kicked.'

'He'd never say that.' Timothy's voice was sharp and urgent.

'Why not?'

'Because it was his idea, he supplied the gear, he ...' He stopped abruptly.

'Don't worry about letting the cat out of the bag. It's only a barrister who, because of a superior code of ethics, is unable to continue to defend a client if guilt is admitted. We solicitors are not expected to act so honourably ... You had no idea Calvin intended to torture and assault Burrell?'

'I didn't even know he had until the police told me.'

'Obviously, they realized this; that is why they offered

167

you the escape route ... Now, we have to decide our future moves.'

'That's obvious,' Rees said. 'Tim changes his plea and tells the truth.'

'As I explained earlier, they've already planted in the jury's mind the fact that Timothy is far fonder of Miss Hurst than is Calvin. In that case, it will seem to them logical to suppose that it must have been Timothy who suggested the operation, Timothy who egged Calvin on to obtaining all the gear, Timothy who administered the violence. So if he now tries to tell the truth, it must appear he is lying at Calvin's expense in order to escape condign punishment.'

'But it's the truth,' Timothy said wildly.

'The truth is what the jury decides is the truth.'

Rees's tone was angry and perplexed. 'Tim knew that if force were used, any confession became inadmissible. So he'd never have made nonsense of the whole object of the exercise.'

'Logically, that has to be so. But the plan was emotionally based. So when he looked down and saw the man he was convinced had raped Miss Hurst, his emotions overwhelmed every last vestige of logic.'

'You sound like the other side.'

'I'm trying to think like the other side; both of them.'

25

Ironically, in the witness box, Burrell engendered a degree of sympathy; for once, his appearance counted more for than against him, since it made him more of a victim, and only the usher, when holding up the card with the oath printed on it, had been close enough to sample the toxicity of his breath.

He gave his evidence well, more sorrowful than indignant that anyone could ever have considered him capable of rape. He related calmly the events of the night of July the ninth and described how the two masked men had demanded he write a false confession admitting rape. When the electrical prod had been applied to his dampened personal (he was too embarrassed to say 'testicle'), he had been convinced that his body was being torn apart . . .

'Did the two intruders frighten you to an equal degree?' Baxter, hands clasped behind his back under his gown, leaned forward so that his ample stomach was against the edge of the reading ledge.

'How's that?' Burrell asked.

'Were you afraid of one more than the other?'

'That's right.'

'Will you tell the court why this should have been?'

'Because it was always the one what used the prod and did all the bashing.'

'From the beginning to the end of your ordeal, it was

one man who either threatened or actually applied torture or violently assaulted you?'

'Yeah.'

'Did the second man give any indication that he either approved or disapproved of what his companion was doing?'

'He didn't stop him, did he?'

'Did he encourage him?'

'Not really,' Burrell said regretfully.

'Did he attempt to discourage him?'

Burrell opened his mouth to answer, closed his mouth.

'If the second man gave the slightest indication of wishing to restrain the actions of the first man, it is your duty to tell the court.'

'Well, it's like he said something.'

'He said what?'

'I can't really remember. I mean, I was so shi . . . I was scared.'

'But he did say something which made you think he was not in favour of the actual use of force on you?'

Creedon stood. 'My Lord, the witness has not testified to any such thoughts.'

The judge looked at counsel over the tops of his spectacles. 'Mr Baxter, I am sufficiently old-fashioned to prefer the witness to give the evidence rather than that his counsel should.'

Baxter, proving that a successful barrister was an actor *manqué*, looked suitably repentant.

Creedon did not have the appearance of an academic; it was in his favour that he looked like a front row forward from Pontypool who thought subtlety was a *double entendre* which had to be explained. Witnesses were very inclined initially to treat him with a measure of contempt. 'Was one man noticeably taller than the other?'

'Can't say he was,' Burrell replied.

'Or noticeably more stockily built?'

'They was the same.'

'Was either left-handed?'

'Can't rightly say. What is this?'

'I am trying to discover if you can positively identify either man by some physical detail since we have heard that they wore similar clothes. But it seems that you cannot. This suggests that the two masked men were sufficiently alike in build and behaviour for it to be virtually impossible for you to distinguish one from the other.'

'I know who was what.'

'Do you? When it has become obvious that had they exchanged places without your knowledge, you would be unable to ascertain from their appearances that this was so?'

'They didn't change.'

'You are convinced that they did not. But earlier, we heard that you were totally terrified – as you had every reason to be. In such circumstances, might you not have missed a great deal of what happened and such memory of events as you have is more impressionistic than factual?'

Christine met them at the front door. 'Well?'

'Burrell's given his evidence,' replied Rees, as he led the way into the hall.

'And?'

'Andrew says he's not done us any more harm. His evidence leaves it open as to who tortured and kicked him.'

'Calvin can still try to claim it was Tim?'

'I'm afraid so.'

'How can anyone be such a bastard?'

'By having a father like his.'

His parents were out to dinner; they'd suggested he join them, but he'd refused. Now, he wasn't so certain that that had been a sensible decision. Admittedly, even ten minutes in Miranda's company weighed heavily, but at least he would not have had to live with his own thoughts . . .

171

The front doorbell rang. Christine had said that Susan might call to pick up the knitting book that was on the table in the hall. Susan was good company. Perhaps she'd stay and have a drink. He went through to the hall and opened the front door to face Penelope.

She was bronzed by the sun and wearing a dress full of colour. He gawped.

'Aren't you going to ask me in? . . . Oh, my God, Tim!' She came forward in a rush and hugged him. 'Mother never told me because she thought it would upset me too much. I didn't know until I saw a mention of the trial in the paper Aunt Kelly bought because there was a reference to her first husband in it. I caught the first plane. Why didn't you tell me?'

'I thought Calvin must have done.'

'Then you must also have thought I didn't give a damn what trouble you were in. You can be a stupid bastard!'

'For those few complimentary words, thank you.'

'How can you have begun to think that if I'd known, I wouldn't come rushing back?'

He sidestepped the question. 'Calvin didn't let you know?'

'Of course not.'

'Why the "of course"?'

She drew back until she could study his face. 'Then he never said anything to you?'

'About what?'

'Now I'm being stupid, to think he ever would. Are you going to offer me a drink?'

'I'm sorry. I'm still shattered by expecting Susan Hawkins and finding you.'

She hugged him tightly once more, finally released him. They went through to the sitting room and she sat on the settee whilst he fetched the drinks. After handing her a glass, he was about to cross to one of the armchairs when she patted the settee. He settled beside her.

'It was entirely Calvin's idea, wasn't it?' she asked.

'Yes.'

172

'And you couldn't realize what a bloody stupid idea it was?'

'It seemed the only way.'

'To what?'

'It doesn't matter.'

'It matters one hell of a lot. Did you follow him just because he told you to? Like you've always done? Like some cowed puppy?'

'That's a beastly thing to say.'

'I don't care. I have to know.'

'I agreed because Calvin told me how you couldn't get over knowing it was Burrell who'd hurt you so terribly yet the police wouldn't arrest him. That every minute of every day, you were terrified by the thought that he might attack you again. That the only way of helping you overcome everything was to get Burrell arrested.'

'When did he say all this?'

'Very soon after you flew to the States.'

'Then you need to know something. When I last saw him, just before I flew, I told him exactly what I thought of him. I said that when I'd desperately needed help, he'd been very careful not to give me any; what had really upset him was not the physical and emotional agony I'd suffered, but that in his eyes I'd become damaged goods; that he was an arrant coward who hadn't the courage to face the truth; that I had as much contempt for him as I had for the rapist.'

'That must explain . . .'

'Explain what?'

'Why he attacked Burrell when he knew that this would make the confession inadmissible. He was never interested in gaining that confession; what he wanted was revenge . . .'

She gripped his hand. 'Revenge for daring to attack me, his property; revenge for what I'd said to him . . .' There was a long silence. 'What's happening at the trial?' she finally asked.

'It's going along quietly.'

'That's not what I was asking?'

'Our chap's reasonably hopeful.'

'You're the worst liar I know. For God's sake, haven't there been enough lies? Tell me the truth.'

He drained his glass. 'There's virtually no hope of either of us getting off. And it looks like Calvin's going to say that it was all my idea and it was I who tortured and kicked Burrell. That should let him escape with a much lighter sentence.'

'Surely your man will prove that that's all balls?'

'He's going to try, but as he says, it won't be easy. Because I visited you in hospital and Calvin didn't, and I saw you at your place more often than he did, it's going to be made to look as if I'm very much fonder of you than he is. Which will persuade the jury that the whole idea was much more likely to have been mine.'

'The sod!' she said bitterly. 'Oh, my God, Tim, I'm so desperately sorry.' She reached out to hug him. .

Her lips were only inches away from his. The scent she was wearing teased his mind. He could feel the swell of her breasts against his chest. Even as part of his mind cursed himself, another part egged him on. He kissed her. Her lips parted and before his tongue could search for hers, hers reached out for his. She took his right hand and brought it up to her breast . . .

They lay on his bed, their naked bodies still moist from love-making.

'I'm sorry,' he said.

She turned on to her side, pressing her body against his. 'That has to be the stupidest thing you'll ever say.'

'But . . . but after what happened . . .'

'You're scared that being raped has made me loathe sex? It did, for a long time. But Aunt Kelly helped me to become far more rational. And when I saw how frightened and miserable you were, and you told me how Calvin was being a complete bastard, I desperately wanted to help. And I knew there was only one way I could. And if you think it was just a case of doing my good deed for the day, it was the most wonderful, the most cloud-twelve screw ever. And you've made me like my body again because it's given both of us such incredible pleasure.'

'I suppose we ought to move,' Timothy said. 'The parents will probably be back soon and they're pre-Reformation when it comes to sex.'

She made no answer and did not move. He sat up and stared down at her and was immediately worried by her expression. 'Is something up?'

'I . . .'

'That last time, I hurt you?'

'Nothing like that. It's just that my mind's suddenly played tricks.'

'How?'

'It's remembered the rape.'

'Oh, God, have I . . . ?'

She pulled him down to herself. 'The memories aren't frightening or making me feel sick; it's as if everything's at second-hand, like watching a video . . . I saw him getting to his feet and dressing. And as he dressed he moved out of the shadow of the wall and I could see a large red mark on his backside which looked rather like Australia . . . To hell with all that. Can't we risk another quarter of an hour and visit Shangri-La again before we become all prim and proper?'

Metcalf walked into the CID general room. 'Did anyone learn if at the time of the rape Burrell had a large red mark, roughly the shape of Australia, on one of his buttocks?'

Naylor said: 'I don't know for sure, sir, but it sounds likely.'

'Why?'

'I asked one of the other electricians why he was called Rudolf since his Christian name's Edward. Seems he was always Rudolf the red-arsed reindeer at school and that name stuck.'

26

Evans said regretfully: 'I'm afraid you're both overlooking something. Whether or not there's now sufficient evidence to arrest Burrell for the rape of Miss Hurst has no direct bearing on this case.'

'It must have,' Rees said harshly.

'Timothy and Calvin are charged with assaulting Burrell. If it can be shown that he was guilty of rape, their motive merely becomes that much stronger.'

'The jury has to be very much more sympathetic.'

'They won't have the chance. Burrell will be questioned again by the police, a medical examination will be held, and the prosecution service will consider the evidence – all that will take weeks. This case will be over within the next two days.'

As his father swore, Timothy wondered bitterly how he could have been so self-deceivingly naïve as to con himself into thinking that there was now hope.

'Naturally, I'll discuss this new evidence with Mr Creedon. He's sharp enough to find out if there is a way of introducing it to your advantage but, realistically, I'm afraid you shouldn't be too hopeful that he'll succeed.'

Daniels could not hide his sharp uneasiness; to the public and the jury he appeared to be just another witness who was embarrassed to be in the limelight, but to others his manner made it obvious that in the past he'd stood in the dock, not the witness box.'You live at number forty-six

176

A, Thorndyke Street, and you were there on the night of the twenty-sixth of June?' Crocker-Smith asked.

'Yes, sir.'

'Was anyone else at that address with you on that night?'

'Mike Fossen.'

'Was he the only other person present?'

'Rudolf turned up.'

'Rudolf?'

'Ted Burrell.'

'Rudolf is Mr Burrell's nickname?' Crocker-Smith sounded relieved. No prosecution counsel, however urbanely competent, welcomed fresh evidence. 'So he was in your house that night. When did he arrive?'

'I don't know exactly.'

'Be as accurate as you can.'

'I suppose it were about ten.'

'And when did he leave?'

'We was listening to music on the telly and then played some CDs. It was late, so he stayed on and didn't leave until the morning.'

'One last question, Mr Daniels. Was Mr Burrell in the house between midnight and one a.m., Sunday morning?'

'That's when we was listening to the CDs.'

'Thank you.' Crocker-Smith sat.

'No questions,' said Baxter, not bothering to stand.

Creedon stood. He studied Daniels for long enough to unsettle the other, finally said: 'Are you an honest man?'

''Course I am.'

'Then the evidence you have just given is the truth?'

'Yes.'

'You are quite certain of that?'

'Mr Creedon,' said the judge, 'I do not like to interrupt counsel, but I must ask if there is any relevance to this line of questioning?'

'Yes, my Lord, there is.'

'The veracity of Mr Burrell's alibi is not at stake.'

'Not directly.'

'Or indirectly,' snapped the judge, who had little time for incompetence and even less for a counsel's attempt to impress a jury with aggressive, irrelevant questions.

'My Lord, I hope to show the court that, on the contrary, indirectly Mr Daniels's evidence concerning Mr Burrell's alibi is of very great consequence to this trial.'

The judge said nothing more, but he promised himself that counsel would hear the rough edge of his tongue if he failed to justify his words.

'Mr Daniels,' said Creedon, 'I will ask you again, are you certain that the evidence you have just given is the truth?'

'Yes.'

'Do you understand what constitutes the offence of perjury?'

Daniels looked round the courtroom as if searching for the nearest exit.

'Perhaps I should remind you. Perjury is the swearing, on oath, to a statement that one knows to be untrue; the giving of evidence, on oath, that one knows to be false. The law rightly regards perjury as very serious and anyone found guilty of it can expect an immediate prison sentence, up to a maximum of seven years. So should it be proved that in this court you have committed perjury, you must expect a heavy prison sentence.'

'I ain't.'

'Are you aware that Miss X was unable to remember many of the details of her rape?'

He shook his head.

'And neither will you know that within the past twenty-four hours, she has suddenly and unexpectedly recovered her full memory. Specifically, she now remembers that on the buttock of her rapist there was a red area which possessed the rough shape of Australia.'

It was obvious that Daniels was beginning to panic.

'Mr Creedon,' said the judge, 'I presume you have good authority for what you have just said?'

'My Lord, Miss X has given the police a sworn statement. I have a copy of that here.'

The usher collected a sheet of paper from Creedon,
carried it to the Bench. The judge read the paper, put it
down. 'Please proceed.'

'Mr Daniels, a birthmark with a distinct shape provides
an excellent means of identification. Therefore, should a
man already a suspect in the case of the rape of Miss X
turn out to possess such a birthmark as she has described,
one may accept that he will be charged and probably be
found guilty of her rape . . . Do you know why Mr Burrell's nickname is Rudolf?'

Daniels shook his head.

'I have been reliably informed that at school he was
known as Rudolf the red-arsed reindeer . . .'

There was some laughter, immediately quelled.

'We know from evidence given in this court that Mr
Burrell was initially a suspect in the case of the rape of
Miss X, but that his alibi, provided by you and Mr Fossen,
seemed to make it certain that he was innocent. Yet if we
now speculate that Mr Burrell's nickname means he has
a red birthmark on his buttock and that this mark pos-
sesses the rough shape of Australia, it has to be certain
that he will be charged with the rape of Miss X and very
probably be found guilty. In this event, it will become
obvious that the evidence you have given here today is
completely false and that you have been guilty of perjury.'

Daniels gripped the edge of the witness box so tightly
that his knuckles whitened.

'Perhaps we should give you one last chance to recon-
sider your evidence. Was Mr Burrell in your house at
half-past midnight on the twenty-sixth of June?'

After a while, he said, 'No,' in little more than a whisper.

'My Lord,' said Creedon, 'it has become clear from the
evidence of Mr Daniels and Mr Fossen that Burrell was
lying when he stated he was in their house at the time of
Miss X's rape. When a witness is shown to have lied on

179

oath about part of his evidence, one must be entitled to assume that much of his other evidence is probably also false. When Burrell claims that two men broke into his house, the true number may have been one or it may have been a dozen. When he claims he was tortured in order to make him write his confession and that that confession was false, it becomes more than probable – since we know the confession was almost certainly true – that he was tortured for an entirely different reason. When he says his assailants had cultivated, BBC English accents, they may well have spoken in broad Glaswegian ones . . .

'My Lord, Burrell's evidence is so central to the case against my client that when his evidence is proved to be wholly untrustworthy, I would submit that my client can have no case to answer . . .'

They stood in the sunshine, hand in hand, waiting for Rees to return from telephoning Christine.

'There you are! I've been searching for you all over the place.'

They turned, to face Calvin.

'By God, your man deserves to be knighted for the way he won the case! Does it call for a celebration! We'll fly to Paris for dinner at the Tour D'Argent and then go on to the new place where the floor show makes the Lido look tatty . . .'

Timothy, Penelope holding his hand even more tightly than before, walked away.